CHASING TEMPTATION

FORBIDDEN SERIES #7

TRACY LORRAINE

A NOTE

Chasing Temptation is written in British English and contains British spelling and grammar. This may appear incorrect to some readers when compared to US English books.

Doing as she asked is harder than I was anticipating. I've never chased a woman in my life. I'm usually the one trying to shake the clingers, but sitting here, waiting for the clock to tick around so I can leave for my class, I wouldn't be opposed to wrapping my arms around her the second I walk into the room and never letting go.

It's been three days since I dropped her off for work on Monday morning, and I've not heard a squeak from her since. I kinda hoped she might at least message me to let me know she's okay, but apparently her need for space meant as much distance as she could put between us as possible.

I can't really argue; she's got shit going on, and

this thing between us has been intense to say the least. She's my teacher, for fuck's sake.

The plan was to re-do a couple of my GCSEs, rewrite a couple of the fuck tonne of mistakes I've made in my life, and see if I'm actually competent enough to consider further education and possibly a serious qualification that might allow me to be more than just a builder.

Okay, so I'm not *just* a builder—my job description says I'm a site agent—but I'm under no illusion that I only got that title because I was in my old boss' back pocket.

I was a mess the day I stumbled into Johnson & Son's office. If the boss had turned out to be anyone but my dad's old mate, I doubt that anyone in their right mind would have given me a job. I was seventeen, covered in tattoos, hungover, and I probably smelled like the back end of a rhino, but he gave me a chance.

Or rather, he gave me what I needed in order for me to do his dirty work.

The second I saw him, I should have known he wasn't offering me a job out of the goodness of his heart. The man had been a friend of my father's; anyone who spent any time with that man was obviously of dubious character. I should have known better than to agree to dance with the devil. It was only later that I was to learn that he was probably worse than my father ever was. He was the master manipulator, and I had no choice but to be his bitch. He could take everything away from me in one swift move if I disobeyed him.

Weirdly, he was the only man I'd listened to in my entire life.

But it wasn't through choice.

It was through necessity.

Looking back now, I can't be all that angry. Yes, he played me, but he wasn't hiding it from me; the person he was really playing was his daughter, Lauren. She's the reason I can't be angry about it all, because he gave me her.

I'd had a few friends growing up but nothing lifelong. The guys at the pretentious all boys private school my parents sent me to only wanted to know me because I knew how to get my hands on alcohol and good weed. Then, when my gran enrolled me into her local comprehensive, I was the bad boy all the 'cool' kids wanted to befriend and all the girls wanted to bed. I certainly got an education from that place, although not in the way of qualifications. I learned that girls would go even further out of their way than boys to get what they wanted, and it was where I discovered that really, I didn't care what sex they were as long as they were willing. I'd lose myself and my shitty life in them in a heartbeat.

I've never been embarrassed by the way I've lived my life or the bad, slutty choices I've made.

Not until I walked into her classroom and her dark, innocent eyes stared into mine. In that moment, I wished everyone I'd ever touched would vanish. She was too good for me, and I was desperate to be worthy. The longer she looked at me, the more I wanted her.

I told myself it was lust at first sight, but even in those very first moments I knew it was more than that. Yes, I wanted to bend her over her desk and fuck her until she cried out my name—that was a given—but more than that I wanted to pull her into my arms and tell her that I'd take away the fear that was oozing from her.

My phone buzzes beside me, and I almost manage to crack a smile at seeing my best friend's picture staring back at me.

Lauren: What time are you showing your face tonight? Erica won't forgive you if you bail.

Tonight's my flat mate's birthday. I do need to be there after everything she's been through recently, but nothing will drag me away from seeing Quinn tonight. I've promised Lauren that I'll get to the restaurant as soon as I can, but I don't think she believes me.

I've kept my Thursday night dalliances to myself. I thought I was crazy when I filled out the application online to go back to school, and I had no idea what those around me would think. Lauren knows about my past, and I've no doubt she'd support me no matter what, but everyone else...I'm not so sure. They don't know what a fuck up I was, and, quite honestly, I'd rather not have to revisit that time in my life.

I reply, promising that I'll be there. What I really want to do is convince Quinn to come with me after class and introduce her to my friends. This thing between us has only been going on for a few days at the most, but already I'm sick of hiding her.

It's still too early to leave but fuck it. I grab my leather jacket and my bag and head out of the flat. I usually take the tube, but seeing as it's pissing it down with rain and with the hope that I'll be able to get Quinn away quicker after class, I unlock the van door and jump in. It's meant to be for business use only, but what's Ben going to do? Fire me? Lauren wouldn't allow it.

One of the benefits of having a bestie who's banging the boss.

I park a little down the street, thinking it'll make Quinn happy later, and slowly make my way inside.

I'm the first to arrive, not that it's a surprise, and her classroom door is shut. I clench and unclench my fists with my need to go barrelling in and pull her into my arms. The fact that she's in the middle of teaching a class is the only thing that stops me. After three days, I'm fucking desperate to feel her body pressed up against mine and to breathe in her sweet scent.

A couple of others I recognise join me. I nod at them in greeting, but no words pass my lips. Befriending my classmates has never been that high up on my to do list. Getting up close and personal with the teacher, though...that one's right up there.

Eventually her class comes to an end and students start filing out of the room. My heart pounds as the anticipation of seeing her gets the better of me.

Shoving my hands in my pockets to stop me from pushing the students leaving the room aside in my haste to get in, I wait as patiently as possible.

When it looks like the last couple of stragglers have left, I take a step forward, beating anyone else to the doorway. They might be keen to learn or whatever, but my need is much more important.

Walking through the doorway, my heart's in my fucking throat. I need to look at her, to stare into her kind, dark eyes and take in her soft curves. I've missed her so fucking much this week and right now, seconds away from laying my eyes on her, I'm not too afraid to admit it.

Dragging in a much needed deep breath, I prepare to look at her—only when I lift my eyes, she's not the one rubbing writing off the white board.

"Where's Miss Smith?" I demand, walking straight to the front of the room. I was concerned about her going home after her flat was broken into. I told myself that I was just being paranoid, but now with her not here, it's sending my imagination into overdrive.

Eddie spins, his eyes narrowing on me, disgust clear within them.

"None of your business. I suggest you take your seat."

"Bullshit. Tell me where she is."

Something flashes in his eyes, and it's enough to tell me that he doesn't know the answer to my demand.

"If she's in trouble and you've done fuck all about it, I'll—"

"I don't know," he admits quietly, his skin paler than it was just a few moments ago.

"You don't... Fuck. When was the last time you saw her?"

"Monday."

"Fuck." My hands go to my hair as I try not to panic. I'm aware I've got a class full of Quinn's students piling in behind me and that Eddie has no clue there's anything between us—or at least he didn't until a few seconds ago. "Did you know her flat was broken into?"

"Y-yes." Guilt twists his features.

"And you didn't think to check up on her, seeing as she hasn't turned up to work since Monday?"

"I meant to, it's just—"

"I don't want your fucking excuses." With that, I turn and march from the classroom. I feel the stares of everyone in the room burning into my back, but I don't care what any of them think or what they might have overheard.

All that matters right now is Quinn.

Please be in your flat. Please be in your flat, I repeat on the drive over. I don't remember any of the journey; my head's too much of a mess with all the things that could have happened. I don't register any traffic lights or roundabouts as I manoeuvre my way through the London traffic. The only thing I know is that I break every single speed limit in my need to get to her.

The second I pull up into her building's car park, I grab the spare keys the locksmith gave me for her flat and jump from the van without bothering to turn the engine off or shut the door. The only thing I can focus on is finding her, and finding her safe.

She's kept her past so close to her chest, but the fear that was always in her eyes and the fact that she was always looking over her shoulder was enough to tell me that she didn't want to come face to face with it again. She tried to play off the break in, but I saw the terror in her eyes. It's the reason I refused to allow her to stay, but it's not like I could have kept her locked up safe after.

She felt the need to come back here, and all I could do was trust her. Fucking wish I hadn't, mind you.

The front door's still fucked when I get to it. I swing it open with such force that it slams back against the wall. If there were any glass still in it, I might be concerned with the force of the collision, but as it is, I don't need to worry.

Taking the stairs three at a time, I race towards her door. I breathe a sigh of relief when I find it closed and locked.

She's just ill inside. She's safe. She'll be there. No matter how many times I repeat those words in my head, I know they're not true. This is bigger than her being so ill she's not phoned into work or let Eddie know. She told me herself that he's her closest friend, so even if she wanted space from me, he should know what's going on with her.

Shoving the first key into the lock, I pray I'll hear her shout, but there's nothing but silence and the sound of the lock releasing. I repeat the action with the other and swing the door open.

My heart's pounding in my chest as I try to make out what's in front of me.

It's pitch black with the curtains pulled shut.

Running my hand along the wall beside me, I

eventually find a switch and bathe the small space in light.

I quickly glance around. Everything's normal. But then I notice something.

The soup and now mouldy bread she left out before our trip at the weekend is still sitting on her coffee table.

Surely she'd have cleaned that up.

I walk over, my eyes darting all over the place to try to piece together what's happened. To my left, I spot her laptop bag dropped randomly on the floor, a pile of papers sliding out of it where it's not zipped up. It's only when I take another step forward that something else catches my eye.

Bending, I run my finger over the spots on the old carpet floor. The colour of the stains has my heart threatening to beat out of my chest. It's fucking blood.

Standing, I back away towards the door.

"What the fuck happened here, Quinn? And where the fuck are you?"

Turning, I slam the door shut behind me and race back in the direction I came. Quinn told me that there's only one person in her present who knows anything about her past. He's the only one who's going to be able to help me right now. I just have to hope she was right and that Eddie is as good a friend as she thought.

THE SHOCK on his face when I storm back into the classroom is even more evident than when I confronted him not even an hour ago.

"She's not fucking there." My voice booms across the room, causing everyone to stop what they're doing and turn my way.

"I'm in the middle of something." Eddie winces at my intrusion, but I see that concern in his eyes again.

"I really don't give a fuck. She's in trouble. You know it as well as I do. But the difference is that you're the only one who knows why and where she might be. Now give these motherfuckers something to keep them busy. You need to start talking."

CHAPTER TWO

My body's vibrating with nervous energy and the need to hurt someone as I wait for Eddie to give my usual class something to keep them entertained. He rushes through his instructions, but I'm not sure how much that's due to his concern or the fact that I'm staring at him with my muscles pulled tight and my fists clenched, ready to fight.

He's made no secret of the fact he doesn't like me, or at least the image I portray. I don't fit into his perfect world of designer suits, pocket squares, and tie pins.

After what feels like a fucking year, he's walking towards me and gestures for me to follow him to his office.

"Where's he taken her, Eddie?" I demand the second he has the door shut.

"I don't know what you're talking about."

"Cut the act. I might only know the very basics, but I know that you know everything. She's been terrified for weeks that he's going to find her, and now she's fucking gone. Where has he taken her?"

"How the fuck should I know? She's been the only one I've had contact with since I left that place."

"But you know where *that place* is. Tell me that. It's got to be a good start."

"Earlington Manor. It's a private school." The name sounds vaguely familiar, but the only private school I know is the hellhole my parents sent me to, and that's not it. "Her father was the head and her husband the head of humanities."

"And why would they want her back?" I need him to fill in a few of my blanks if I have any chance of understanding what the fuck is going on right now.

"Have you not seen the news recently?"

I cast my mind back to the image of Quinn freaking out in our hotel room while I was watching the news.

"Earlington Manor," I say out loud, more to myself than Eddie. "Sex scandal, child abuse, massive enquiry—"

"The one and only. She exposed them. Managed to get evidence that her dad covered up one of her husband's most recent indiscretions and went to the police with it. Then she ran."

"Fuck."

I fall down onto the chair behind me as the information sinks in.

It makes so much sense. It's why she was so against us. She thought that by being with me, she was becoming them.

"Fuck," I repeat, not quite believing what I'm hearing but knowing full well that it's true.

"That place was hell on earth. A place full of wealth where money can buy anything and any wrongdoing can be covered up without a second thought."

"Where is it? We need to go there. We need to find her."

"We?"

"Yes, motherfucker. *We*. Don't you care about her? She told me you were her only friend. Don't you want to know she's safe as much as I do?"

"Yes but—"

"But what? Please don't tell me that you're too much of a stuck-up, pocket square wearing prick to get your hands dirty to save her."

"Uh…"

"Fuck this. I'll Google it. I'll get to her with or without your help."

Turning away from him, I wrench the door open with enough force that it could well come off its hinges before running out of the building and towards where I abandoned my van on the double yellow lines out the front of the college.

By some fucking miracle I've not got a ticket—not that it's my biggest concern right now.

Pulling my phone from my pocket, I type in the school name Eddie just gave me and immediately news headlines light up my screen.

Head teacher covering for his own and his teacher's child abuse.
Lies, betrayal, and abuse uncovered.
Hundreds of victims of abuse at Earlington Manor are coming forward.

"Jesus," I mutter. No wonder she wanted nothing more to do with the place.

Eventually I manage to find the school's

website amongst all the news sites, and I locate the postcode at the bottom of the homepage.

Lake District. Nothing like making it easy for me.

Plugging it into my SatNav, I wait for it to find the location and balk when I see the estimated time.

Five motherfucking hours.

"Sorry, Erica, but this is way more important," I say into the small space around me before slamming my foot down on the accelerator and flying into the middle lane, much to the other drivers' annoyance.

It takes me forever to get out of the city and onto the motorway. The SatNav's telling me that I won't be there until gone midnight. I desperately want to go storming in and rescue my girl, but the reality of the situation is that the only address I have is that of a school, and the chance of her being there is probably pretty slim.

It's the longest drive of my life. By the time I pass the 'Welcome to the Lake District' sign, my entire body is locked up with tension. I need to let off some steam but anything less than ploughing my fist into Quinn's ex-husband won't suffice. He's been harassing her from a distance for weeks. It's time he got a taste of his own medicine.

The winding country roads are seemingly endless, but eventually, just as I hit the crest of a hill, this huge old manor house comes into view.

"Wow, pretentious," I mutter as I drive through the entrance, surprised that I'm not stopped by giant gilded gates. They'd fit right in.

Parking up, I climb from the van and stretch out my sore muscles. Huge spotlights illuminate the grand building, and I'm under no illusion that I'm probably the focus of a million CCTV cameras right now, but still, I can't help walking up to the closest window and peeking inside. It's an office. A huge mahogany desk sits in the centre with a massive computer screen on the top. There are a few filing cabinets and an antique looking chair pushed behind the desk but nothing that helps me out with my little quest.

The sound of a barking dog forces me back into my van. The last thing I need is to be wrestled to the ground by a guard dog.

Driving away from the school, I do a tour of the local village. The houses are beyond huge; I guess they would be if they could afford for their kids to go to an establishment like that. I wonder how all the parents feel, watching the news stories play out, knowing the amount of money they've spent to send their little angel to be cared for by a bunch of paedophiles. A shudder runs down my spine. I hated my time at private school, but I never experienced or was aware of that kind of treatment from the teachers. The only kind of thing they could ever be accused of would be turning the other cheek at all the things we got up to.

There's no evidence of life or even a bed and breakfast, so when I come to the decision that I'm at a bit of a dead end, I pull over in a dark layby and tip my chair back as far as it will go in the hope that I might get a bit of sleep. I know it's wishful thinking. As I lie there, all kinds of images run through my head about where she could be or what could be happening to her. If her husband, and her dad for that fact, don't bat an eyelid at hurting innocent kids then they're not going to think twice about punishing Quinn for going against them, that I'm positive of.

I tried her phone on the drive up here. I was in two minds in case he's got it and is monitoring her calls, but my need to find out got the better of me. I was proven wrong about him sitting there waiting for it to ring, because it didn't even go to voicemail.

CHAPTER THREE

I'm still awake when the sun starts to rise over the hills in the distance, and I'm still none the wiser as to what to do. I could start knocking on doors, but if this little community is as tightknit as I imagine it to be then I'll totally lose the element of surprise. Quinn can't have been the only one who knew about the goings on inside that school building, so my guess is that everyone around here is either stupidly loyal or as dodgy as the men in Quinn's life.

Putting my seat back up, I grab my phone and find a message from an unknown number.

Swiping it open, I find an address staring back at me. My brows draw together until I see that the address is for a house in this village.

A small smile of achievement twitches at the corner of my lips that Eddie does care after all. Maybe he really is the kind of guy Quinn thinks he is. Putting it into the SatNav, I find that it's only three minutes away.

I'm sitting out the front of what I assume is Quinn's old marital home before I get a chance to blink. It's a million miles away from her flat in London and just seeing the sheer size of the place helps me to understand her that little bit more.

She must have left everything behind when she ran. Well, everything aside from those damn twinsets. Even those make sense now. I bet it's all the women wear around here—that and a set of pearls around their necks while their husbands are up to all sorts.

Disgust curls at my lips at what's been happening here for probably longer than anyone wants to admit.

I sit and watch the house for a while. It's silent. The only clue that someone might be home is that there's a Porsche and an Audi parked in the driveway. I don't particularly want to sit out here all day. It's going to become seriously fucking obvious that I'm watching the place soon.

My stomach rumbles, reminding me that I

didn't eat for most of yesterday due to the intended swanky meal for Erica's birthday, so I decide to try to find somewhere to get some food and come back later. Thankfully it gets dark pretty early these days—plus it's grey, raining, and foggy up here. I'll be much more inconspicuous under a cloud of darkness.

"WHAT THE FUCK is going on, Joe?" Lauren shrieks at me when I tell her that I'm not going to be at work today. I'm sitting at a table in the first cafe I found about twenty minutes from the village.

I let out a large sigh. I don't have a fucking clue where to start.

"You're really starting to worry me." Her words make my heart hurt. For a long time, Lauren was the single most important person in my life. The day I stumbled into Johnson and Son's offices in the hope of finding a job, I didn't think my entire life would change.

Okay, so her cuntbag of a dad basically blackmailed me into befriending her, but that was never my reason for truly wanting to spend time with her. The second I spotted her sitting behind her desk, looking like someone had just run over her puppy, something called to me. I was drawn to her in a way I've never been with anybody else ever, until Quinn. There was even a time, not all that long ago actually, that I thought there could have been more between us. She was my rock, she had been for years, and my broken heart got a little carried away with itself. Watching her hooking up with the guy who'd put that sad look on her face the day I first met her was a bit of a slap across the face. I was under the stupid illusion that she was mine, and it hurt having the guy who basically brought us together swoop in and steal her from under my feet.

It didn't take me all that long to realise that I was living in a fantasy land. She was never mine to have. She was my best friend, and when I really thought about that, it was exactly what I wanted. What I *needed*. It wasn't until I fell for Quinn that I realised that what I felt for Lauren wasn't real. The love I had for her was as my best friend. It wasn't real love. I was yet to feel that back then.

But now? Now I've had a taste of how incredible that can be, and like fuck am I allowing it to slip through my fingers.

"I've...uh...I've met someone," I admit for the

first time. I've kept Quinn a secret, mainly because I knew it was what she wanted. She was right every time she told me that we shouldn't have been doing what we were, because the facts of it are that we're student and teacher, no matter my age. It'll still be seen that she's taking advantage of her position and she'll be the one in the wrong, no matter how much I might have chased her. But also, I was worried that if everyone knew, if I even mentioned it, then it might not be real. Crazy, I know, but I'd found this little burning light, something I didn't know I needed until the moment I laid eyes on her, and I didn't want to ruin it by having my friends nosing in on my business.

A loud shriek comes through the phone. "Shut the fuck up. You have not. Where? Who is it? Name? When can I meet them?" she asks, exactly as I expected her to. In all the time we've been friends and even living together, I've never once mentioned someone of any significance in my life. This must be somewhat of a shock.

"One step at a time, yeah. I'll tell you all that stuff when I'm back—"

"Where the hell are you?" she interrupts.

I let out a long, pained breath. "She's got some

shit going on with people from her past. I'm...uh...trying to smooth the situation over."

"You...playing peacekeeper. Now that I'd pay to see." She laughs, and my stomach drops to my feet. If only it were that simple. "I hope they're expecting a bad boy with ink to show up or you could be in trouble."

I refrain from telling her that my art of choice isn't really an issue right now, but I don't want to drag her into this. It's bad enough that Quinn's in the middle of it.

"Things are...complicated. I'd really appreciate it if you'd keep this to yourself for now, but I promise that as soon as I can, I'll tell you everything you want to know and I'll even let you meet her."

"You'll let me? Wow, I feel so privileged." Sarcasm drips from her words, but I can't care right now. I've got bigger issues than pissing off my best friend.

"Listen, I've got to go. I'll call you when I can, just tell Ben I've got the shits or something, yeah?"

"I've got you, just..." she hesitates, and I hold my breath, waiting for what's going to come next. "Just don't make me regret it."

"I won't. Love you."

"Hmmm... You too. Bye."

I hang up just as the waitress I saw heading this way places a huge plate of fried breakfast down in front of me. I thought I was hungry, but staring down at it after having talked about Quinn, even just briefly with Lauren, killed my appetite somewhat.

I waste the day driving around. I fill up the van just in case we need to make a quick getaway and basically just wait until the sun sets. The second the sky turns dark, I make my way back towards the address Eddie supplied me with.

I've not heard any more from him since that message, so I assume he's been busy teaching all day and trying to ignore what could be happening here. He didn't seem all that keen to get involved yesterday, so I don't know why I'm surprised.

It's completely dark when I pull up behind another car that's parked in the layby I found opposite the house earlier. Pulling my black work hoodie from behind my seat, I drag it over my head and keep the hood up before getting out.

The frozen grass crunches under foot and my breaths come out in clouds of white around me as I make my way towards the house. There are lights on inside, but I see no movement.

Avoiding the stoned driveway, knowing the sound of my footsteps could tip off anyone inside, I make my way around the side of the house.

Looking into a small window, all I can see is the hallway and a couple of doors. Really not helpful. I need to know where she is and if she's okay, not how she decorated her old house.

Blowing out a frustrated breath, I continue towards the back of the house until a twig snapping up ahead catches my attention and my heart jumps into my throat, but when a figure steps out from the trees, I realise that I vaguely recognise his stance.

"What the fuck?" I ask, marching towards him.

"You were right. We need to make sure she's okay."

"And here I was, thinking you were a stuck-up pussy."

Eddie fumes at my words but wisely keeps his mouth shut. He must be well aware that's how he came across yesterday when he basically sent me on my mission without even a good luck thrown my way.

"I'm hoping you have a plan."

The light coming on in an upstairs bedroom

halts our conversation, but almost as soon as it's switched on, it's off again.

"Not really. If I walk up and say, 'Hello mate, let's go and get a pint,' he's going to see straight through me. I hated him when I was here, and the feeling was very much mutual, especially when he found out I'd befriended his wife. Apparently she was his and his alone. He's a control freak. Whatever he's up to will have been well planned, but—"

"There'd better be something positive coming next," I mutter.

"But it also means he's a creature of habit, so he'll have some kind of routine."

"Like?"

"Like Friday night was poker night at the school."

A smile twitches at my lips. We might have a chance at an empty house.

"What time?"

"Eight, but he always got there early to help set up. Arse licker," he adds, making me want to laugh because I can picture him doing the exact same thing.

"I guess we'd better get comfortable." I rest back against a tree, my eyes locked on the house, hoping for some movement or a clue as to whether she's inside.

"What, you're not going to storm the place anyway?"

"I'm not a fucking Neanderthal. I'd rather find a way to get us all out of this alive if possible." The mention of anyone dying sends a shiver down my spine. The bloke's a paedophile and an abuser... surely he's not a murderer as well, right?

"Do you think he'd really hurt her?" I ask hesitantly when my last comment fades into the darkness around us.

"I wouldn't put anything past him. He's hurt her before."

Something explodes in my stomach and races through my veins. "He what?" I roar, a little too loudly seeing as we're meant to be hiding.

"Look, I don't know any details, and he was always careful to keep the bruises hidden—not that that was hard, seeing as she was expected to dress like a nun." *The fucking twinsets.*

My fists clench with my need to end this man. How dare he lay a hand not only on innocent kids but on Quinn. *My* Quinn.

"Calm down," Eddie demands when he gets a look at my expression and the heaving of my chest.

"We need to go about this rationally. You getting all angry and possessive isn't going to help us."

"I'm sorry, I didn't realise you were experienced with this kind of thing." He opens his mouth to respond but obviously changes his mind. "Lucky for us, I know a thing or two about breaking and entering."

"Of course you do," he mutters, but I choose to ignore it. I know how I look, and I know how I'm judged by people like him.

Silence falls around us as we watch and wait. The minutes tick by painfully slowly. The light from the window we saw earlier flicks on and off a few more times before movement downstairs captures my focus. I want to see the motherfucker who's going to rot in jail after this. I want to look him in the motherfucking eyes until he knows that what he tried to ruin is now mine, and like fuck am I ever going to treat her like he did.

"I think he's going," Eddie whispers, his own eyes locked on the house.

"What gave you that idea?" I quip, seeing as we've both just watched him shrug his coat on.

"Fuck off. Do you want my help or not?"

Rolling my eyes, I turn my focus back to the house. We can't see the front door, but we hear it slam and then the engine of one of the cars roaring to life.

"Ready?" Eddie asks, but he's too late. I'm already halfway towards the house.

Pulling my sleeve down over my hand, I slam it through the glass in the outbuilding and reach inside for the handle.

"What the fuck? This place is alarmed."

"That old thing strapped to the front of the house? Please, that stopped working years ago."

I push the door open, and he follows me until we reach another.

"Now what?"

"Do you have any confidence in me?"

He mutters a response, but I don't hear it. I'm too busy backing up, ready to slam my shoulder into the wood and hoping it's as weak as it looks.

"Joe, I don't think that's—" A loud crash sounds out as the door comes free from its hinges and falls into the kitchen beyond.

"Shut the fuck up, posh boy. Are you actually going to help me or just stand there looking like you're going to piss your pants?"

He fumes, looking over my shoulder. "You go. I'll keep watch."

I'm on the move before he even finishes his sentence.

The house is a blur as I run through to find the stairs. I know exactly where I need to go; I just need to find out how to get there.

Taking the stairs three at a time, I race towards the back of the house. Door after door lines the long hallway, making the house seem so much bigger than it looked from the outside.

I throw each one open and find the light, but each one is empty aside from the furniture. That is, until I get to the one at the very end. When I turn the handle, nothing happens.

"Quinn?" I roar, hoping to get a response, but nothing other than the sound of my own erratic breathing fills my ears. "Fuck."

Backing up, I run at the door, hoping it's as useless as the one downstairs. Sadly, it isn't, and it's not until my third attempt that the wood starts to splinter. I put everything I have into the fourth shove, and thankfully, the door swings open at a twisted angle.

The room is in darkness and the windows have been closed up for some time, if the musty smell is anything to go by.

A noise—a moan—breaks through the ringing

in my ears, and when I slam my hand down on the light switch, the woman it belongs to comes into focus but only barely, the dim bulb hanging in the centre of the room dull at best.

"Quinn, fuck." Running towards her, I drop to my knees beside her lifeless body. My heart aches in my chest; it damn near feels like it's going to split in two as I stare down at her.

There's a dirty rag wrapped around her face, cutting into her mouth, halting her from speaking. I make quick work of untying it and pulling her weak body into my arms.

Quiet sobs fall from her lips as she shivers against me.

"It's okay. You're safe now. I've got you." Her body is limp in my arms. She's exhausted; clearly she's been locked in here for a few days. "I'm going to get you out of here."

I push to stand with her wrapped tightly in my arms, but I don't get to full height.

Dropping back to my knees, I lift the blanket covering her to find that her wrists and ankles are bound together, the rope around her delicate skin then tied to huge hooks in the floor.

"Motherfucker."

Gently lowering her, I search for something to

cut the rope with. Coming up empty, I realise I'm going to have to leave her. My stomach turns over at the thought of her being alone in here once again.

"I'll be right back and we'll get you out of here." As I gently caress her cheek, her tears wet my fingers as I stare into her blue...wait, blue eyes? She moans in pain, pulling my focus. Releasing my hold on her, I race to the door and back to the kitchen. My heart pounds, my legs not able to move me as quickly as I want to go.

Eddie's nowhere to be seen, but his disappearance doesn't even really register. My entire world is tied up upstairs, and I can't think of anything aside from getting her away from here. There's a knife rack on the counter, I pull out what I hope will be the sharpest of the set and race back to Quinn.

"I'm going to get you out of here, babe. It's all going to be okay."

My harsh breathing fills the room as I saw through the rope keeping her here. My heart's in my throat as images of me walking out with her in my arms fill my mind. I'm going to take her home and keep her safe. She's never going to have to worry about this lunatic ever again.

The knife slides through the rope at her feet before I start work on her hands. I'm just about to cut through the last few fibres when a whimper rumbles up her throat, her eyes going wide in fear.

I turn to look at what has her attention before something hard slams into my head and I'm knocked off my feet. The knife falls from my hand, clattering to the wooden floor at my side. Everything goes fuzzy. Darkness threatens to consume me as I look up to the person yielding a baseball bat.

"She doesn't deserve to be rescued. Elizabeth's nothing more than a filthy whore."

"Motherfucker." By some miracle, my body follows orders despite the burning pain in my head, and I jump to my feet. I use his shock to my advantage to get a good look at him. He's dressed like he should be heading to a golf club, not a fucking poker match, with his jumper tied over his shoulders.

He's not expecting me to get up so easily, and his eyes widen in shock. I step towards him, the muscles in my neck straining, the need to feel him break beneath my bare hands all-consuming.

I'm on him before he's even had time to blink,

but I'm already on the back foot with my head swimming.

I get a few solid punches in before he manages to duck around the side of me. My vision's still blurry at the edges, and it seems like it takes forever to turn around and see where he's gone. If he's touching her, I swear to god I'll kill the motherfucker.

"Joe," Quinn's bloodcurdling scream fills my ears and makes me move a little faster, but it's too late. The knife I was using to free her is firmly in his hand and he's moving towards me faster than I can compute. I don't feel anything as the cold metal cuts into my abdomen, but I do hear Quinn's continued screams filling the room.

I don't feel anything until he pulls the knife from my body, then the pain hits.

A roar fills my ears, and it's not until I find myself flying at him that I realise the noise actually came from me.

I see red and take him down to the floor, my fists pounding into his face over and over. The need to end this motherfucker is all I can think about. A red haze descends on me like I haven't felt in years, and I find myself totally out of control. I've no idea how much time passes as I lay into him. He has no chance of fighting me off. I'm like a man possessed as blood sprays from his face and his ribs fracture under my force.

It's not until a pair of hands land on my shoulders that I'm dragged from the moment.

I spin, my fist ready to continue fighting, but I falter when I find a copper standing behind me.

"I think you can stop. He seems to have got just a little bit of what he deserves," he says with a wink. More amusement fills his voice than it probably should, given the situation.

Looking behind him, I find Eddie standing in the doorway with blood running from his lip and an already swollen eye. He looks between me and something behind me, and it's then that reality comes back.

"Quinn, fuck." I run over, falling to my knees at her side and pulling her to me. I'm amazed the coppers allow it, but when I look back one of them nods at me, a small smile on his lips. It's only as I wrap my arms around her and the blanket falls away from her trembling body that I realise she's naked beneath.

I don't care that the man who did this is currently unconscious on the other side of the room. The knowledge that he might have touched what's mine makes me want to do it all over again.

She must sense where my thoughts are, because her cold hand lands on the side of my neck.

"It's done. It's over." Her voice is weak at best. She needs a hospital, that much is obvious, but as paramedics rush into the room, the last thing I want to do is let her out of my arms.

I hold her tighter to me as they tend to *his* body and wheel him out on a gurney, although admittedly they don't put a lot of care into their actions.

"Shit." Quinn's soft, concerned voice fills my ears as she lifts her hand from my side. It's bright red and the reminder I need about the knife. The sight of my own blood on her hand makes me feel a little queasy.

"I'm fine. It's just a scratch." It's a lie, and we both know it.

I shift us so I can rest my head back against the wall and keep her tightly in my arms. I'm vaguely aware of voices in front of us, but I can't make out any words.

My limbs feel heavy, but that doesn't mean I'm

going to let Quinn go. I've got her back now, and I'm never letting her out of my sight again.

I fight the darkness that wants to consume me, but eventually I lose and everything fades. A weight is lifted from me as I'm totally consumed by darkness. Her blue eyes and soft curves fill my mind, and I just about remember thinking that there could be a worse way to go.

CHAPTER FOUR

Beeping is the first thing I notice before the ache that starts somewhere in the middle of my body and radiates out to the very tips of my fingers and toes. What the fuck is—*shit.*

I can hear movement in the distance, but as I try to figure out what it all means, darkness claims me once again.

I've no idea how much time passes before my senses come back to me once again, but when they do, a few memories hit me.

Quinn.

Before I manage to even attempt to drag my eyes open, I'm out cold again.

The next time I come to, I hear a vaguely familiar male voice.

"I hate leaving you like this, but I've got to get back."

"It's fine, I get it. I'm fine." Quinn. My heart aches at hearing her voice, and I want more than anything to be able to look at her, but my eyes won't cooperate.

"I know you are, and so is he." My skin heats, knowing they're looking at me.

"I-I know." Quinn sniffles, and it breaks my heart that she's hurting.

"You heard the doctor. He was lucky and will be back to his usual self soon. Plus those two dodgy coppers have somehow managed to ensure there's no investigation so he's in the clear." I'm not sure if Eddie is happy about that or not, but as long as Quinn is, that's all that matters.

"I know." Her quiet sobs fill the room, but the darkness starts to claim me once again.

The next time I come to it's quiet, aside from the fucking beep, and I panic.

Quinn.

My need to know if she's okay has me trying to move.

"Argh," I cry as I try to sit up, my eyes flying open for the first time. The electric lights above me burn, making me squint as I attempt to curl myself into a ball in the hope that the pain stops.

"It's okay, just relax." The sound of her soft voice calms me down instantly, and the warmth of her hand landing on my cheek makes every tense muscle in my body relax.

"Quinn?" My throat is so dry that her name is barely audible. My eyes crack open and her blurry face fills them.

"Shhh. I'm here."

Her other hand squeezes mine, and it's enough for me to relax and drift back off to sleep.

I have no idea where I am or how I got here, but she's beside me. That's all that matters.

The next time I come to, the pain has subsided slightly, but the most obvious difference is that there are two female voices softly speaking, both of which I recognise.

"I can't believe he turned up like that expecting just to walk out with me."

"I can. He's pretty hard headed. Once he gets an idea he doesn't generally stop until he gets what he wants."

"Damn fucking straight." My voice is rough and my throat burns as I say the words, but I can't lie here listening to them talk about me.

Silence falls around us, but I'm yet to open my eyes, seeing as my eyelids feel like lead weights, but I know they're there, and I know they're both staring at me.

Both of my hands are grasped.

"Don't you ever do that to me again, you hear me?" Lauren chastises, squeezing my hand tighter.

Mustering up as much strength as I can find, I drag my eyes open to look at her.

Concern and exhaustion covers her face, her brows pulled tightly together.

"If you hadn't just come out of surgery, I'd put you in there myself for scaring me like that."

"Wha—"

"Here, have some water." Looking to my left, I find Quinn holding out a plastic cup with a straw.

She looks beautiful. She always will to me, but it's clear to see that she's been through a harrowing experience. She has huge, dark circles under her eyes. Her skin is a pale grey colour, and her cheeks look a little sunken. But it's the cut lip and the angry bruise high up on her cheekbone that have a burning need for revenge raging through my body. The thought of what he could have done to her in that dark room has the little contents of my stomach threatening to make themselves known.

"Not now," she whispers, her eyes pleading with mine to let it go. She can clearly read my thoughts, making me wish I could read everything she's feeling in this moment, but my head's too fuzzy to know my own thoughts let alone hers.

After drinking the entire cup, I turn back to my best friend. "Not that I'm not happy to see you, but why are you here?"

"Nice," she says with a laugh. "I'm your next of kin. I got a phone call to say you'd been stabbed and I damn near crapped my pants. Why didn't you tell me about any of this?" She gestures to Quinn, and I immediately feel terrible for shutting her out of this part of my life.

"I did. I told you...this morning?"

"Friday morning," she says after looking at her watch. "That was probably a little late though, don't you think?"

I shrug. Quinn was a huge part of my reason for keeping us secret, and I'd go to the ends of the earth to protect her. I hope I'd proved that.

Quinn sits silently beside me. Her hand might be in mine, but with her legs curled up under her in as small a ball as she can manage, she looks more closed off than I've ever seen her. I want to pull her into my arms and never let her go, but even turning to look at her fucking hurts.

A firm knock sounds out in the small room before a young female police officer pokes her head in.

"Good to see you awake, Mr. Kingsman." A small smile twitches at her mouth before she turns to Quinn. "Could we have a chat please, Ms. Davenport?"

My brows draw together. *Davenport?*

Quinn uncurls her legs and stands. It's then that I really see what her few days captive have done to her. The pair of leggings she's wearing are hanging off her, and the hoodie's hanging loosely from her shoulders. How is that possible after such a short amount of time?

I'm too confused by everything as she kisses my forehead and follows the copper from the room. My head spins with the hazy memories of what happened for me to end up here.

"What did she just call Quinn?"

"Ms. Davenport. Why?"

The name Elizabeth pops into my head for some reason, but I can't pinpoint why.

"N-nothing." I'm too confused to even attempt to make any sense of it.

There's another knock on the door and I'm forced to push my thoughts aside as a doctor and a nurse make their way into the room.

"Mr. Kingsman, it's so good to finally see those eyes," the nurse coos softly. Her tone makes my spine stiffen. I don't need anyone to talk to me like a fucking child.

"I'm just going to go and grab a coffee. Let you do your thing. I'll be back soon." Lauren squeezes my hand and mouths 'be good' before slipping from the room. As if I'd be anything but. I roll my eyes at her retreating form before glancing back at the patronising nurse.

She pulls the clipboard from the base of my bed and starts taking notes while the doctor questions me about my pain levels and checks the lines in the back of my hand, which I only now notice are attached to bags of blood hanging above my head.

He must see where my attention is because he starts explaining.

"You lost a lot of blood before you got here, but hopefully by the time this bag is done you won't need any more. The stab wound could have done some real damage to your bowel, so we had to open you up and assess the situation. I'm pleased to say it really could have been a lot worse. You were relatively lucky, Mr. Kingsman."

Lucky? I was stabbed by a psychopath who locked up my girl like his fucking prisoner. The memory hits me like a fucking sledgehammer.

The machine beside me starts beeping incessantly.

"You really need to stay calm, Mr. Ki—"

"It's Joe," I bark, hating being called by my surname unless it's coming from Quinn. It's the only thing I still have that connects me to my parents, and I fucking hate it.

"Sure. Please, try not to get worked up. We'd like to get you out of this place as soon as possible, so just sit back, relax, and let us take care of you."

I've only been conscious briefly, and already I fucking hate this. No one's looked after me since I was a child. Okay, so maybe that's not totally true. I did get the flu a couple of years ago and Lauren played the part of nurse perfectly. She humoured me with my ridiculous demands but drew the line when I asked for a couple of strippers to come and keep me company while she was at work. I thought she was being a spoilsport; she said she was concerned about my blood pressure while being so ill, which seems to be a thing if the nurse's recent words are anything to go by. My granddad and my dad had dodgy tickers, so I guess I should be a little careful seeing as it's hereditary.

I lie there, getting more and more pissed off as they poke, prod, and ask me a million and one questions. Apparently I'm expected to stay in this shithole for a week at least as I recover from both the transfusions and surgery.

There's no fucking way that's happening.

I don't know where I am. I've no idea if Quinn is okay after everything she's been through. Fuck, I don't even really know *what* she's been through. I've got the barest of details about what happened with her dad and ex-husband. I need to get her out of here and somewhere safe so she can recuperate and figure out a way to rebuild her life.

After what feels like a fucking week, the rock hard pillows have been fluffed, the rough bed sheets are neatly tucked around me, and I'm finally left alone with someone else's blood slowly dripping into my body,

I. Fucking. Hate. It.

I lie there alone with only the sounds of the machines around me for company as I try to drag up as many memories from that night as possible. I must try so hard that I wear myself out, because soon everything fades once again and I float off into dreamland.

When I wake again, the lights are dimmed, although I can still see every inch of the room. The first thing I notice is that the beeping is no more. I look to see if I'm no longer attached to the irritating machine, but before I find that my eyes land on Quinn.

She's curled up in the reclining chair with a hospital pillow tucked under her head and her cheek resting on her hand. Her dark hair is all over the place, nothing like it usually is, and her skin is almost grey. I hate that I'm stuck in this bed and unable to comfort her after whatever it was she endured at that monster's hand. She's dressed in the same pair of leggings and hoodie as earlier. The only bit of skin she's showing is her face, and I hate that she's hiding once again.

It occurs to me that that was what the twinsets were. They covered as much skin as possible and made her blend into the crowd, or at least with every other woman I would imagine were in their circle of friends. Her choices of the short leather skirts and the flared dresses make so much sense. *I* make so much sense. She was rebelling from the life she had before, the life she hated. Was she just with me because I was the rebel to help her break free? What happens now? My heart begins to race as I consider that the strength of my feelings might not be reciprocated. I'm not sure how I'll cope if she tells me it was just a bit of fun and that now her ex-douchebag and father have been locked up where they belong, she's going back to her old life, her old job.

I'm on the cusp of what I can only assume is my first ever panic attack when the door opens and a friendly looking nurse comes walking in. She's slightly on the podgy side, her uniform clinging to her hips and arse a little too tightly, but she has the kindest face I think I've ever seen.

"Good evening, sweetie. I'm Shelly," she whispers, noticing Quinn sleeping in the chair beside me. "How are you feeling?"

"Frustrated. When can I get out of this fucking bed?"

She chuckles at my irritation. "You'll soon be up on your feet like it never happened."

"Not soon enough," I grunt.

"You remind me of my son. He's just as hot headed." She potters around, checking my vitals.

"Yeah? He must be pretty awesome."

"He is. He also wouldn't think twice about

running in and saving the girl he loves." Her eyes flick over to Quinn, and I can't help but follow.

Her lips are now parted. She looks so peaceful, and I pray that whatever happened to her escapes her in her slumber. I know it hasn't always been the case.

"She's refused to leave your side, you know? We all thought we were going to have to get her scrubbed up to go into theatre with you." She laughs. "Somehow we managed to convince her to let us see to her while they were working on you. You've got a good one there, boy."

My heart pounds against my ribs. Is what she's saying true? If it is, it makes my earlier concern seem a little pointless. Is Quinn just sticking around because she feels guilty that she dragged me into her mess, or is she really here because she wants to be? I guess only time will tell.

I fall silent, my mind wandering back to the events that put us both in here. I know I can't remember everything, but his face is one thing I'm pretty sure I'll never forget.

"Shelly?" I ask as she wraps a blood pressure band around my arm.

"Yeah?"

"Do you know what happened to the man who put me in here?"

"You mean the man you also put in here?" she jokes lightly. "I'm sorry, Joe. I'm not allowed to discuss other patients' conditions."

"He's alive then. What a shame." She gives me a weak smile, but if she knows even just a little of the detail around what happened, I can't help but think she probably agrees with me. "There was another man too," I say, thinking about Eddie being there.

"He's fine. Sent home with nothing more than a butterfly stitch on his eyebrow." I nod. At least someone got out of this unscathed.

CHAPTER FIVE

When I wake again, the lights are glowing above my head and Quinn is stirring beside me.

I watch as her eyelids flicker open and she stretches her neck, proving just how uncomfortable it must be sleeping in that chair.

"Morning, beautiful," I whisper, not wanting to scare her seeing as she's not looked up at me yet.

Her tired eyes find mine and my heart aches that she feels the need to put herself second right now. She needs to recover just as much if not more than me after everything she went through.

"How are you feeling?" She swings her legs from the chair and leans towards the bed so she can take my hand in hers.

"Ready to leave."

A small smile curls at the corner of her lips, and I will it to continue. Seeing her wide, genuine smile would go a long way to making me feel normal right now. "You're so predictable."

"How's that?"

"I told your first nurse I saw that I had a feeling you'd be a nightmare patient."

"That's harsh, Quinn. Whatever gave you that idea?"

"I just didn't have you down as the kind of man who lies back and takes what's coming to him."

"Well." A suggestive smirk plays on my lips. "That all depends on the situation, doesn't it? I'd gladly lie back and take whatever *you* had to give me."

Her cheeks heat and my cock stirs beneath the thin sheet covering me, despite my slightly broken body. "Joe, you can't—"

"Okay, kids. Stop getting the patient excited," Shelly says with a laugh as she wanders in with a tray of pills for me.

"I'm just going to use the bathroom."

Quinn gets up and I panic, not wanting to watch her walk from the room. For the first time since I woke up, my body responds properly when I try to move, and I manage to wrap my fingers around her wrist before she gets away. Only, her response to my touch isn't what I was hoping for.

She gasps and rips her arm from my fingers, holding it across her body like I just burned her. Her eyes fill with tears before she runs from the room.

"Shit. Fuck." Throwing myself back onto the bed, my hands scrub down my rough face.

"She's been through a lot, sweetie. Just give her a little time. Do you feel up to having a go at getting to your feet? If you are, we could get you into the shower." The image her words conjure up are incredibly attractive because my skin feels disgusting, but I hate the idea of being forced away from Quinn longer than necessary.

"As long as we're fast. I don't want to leave her."

Shelly smiles, biting back the words that are clearly on the tip of her tongue.

I don't think I've ever truly appreciated being able to stand up, but after being in a bed for god knows how long, I'm really fucking thankful as my feet just about shuffle me towards the adjoining bathroom. The fact that Quinn didn't come in here makes me worry even more about where her head's at right now.

The short walk to the bathroom, even with Shelly supporting me, is the hardest fucking walk of my life. My stomach aches where the motherfucker stabbed me. I expect that but not for my legs not to work. It gives me a bit of a clue as to why they want me to stay here for a week. It also gives me even more of a push to prove them wrong and get out of here at the first opportunity. And when I leave, I'm walking out of those motherfucking doors with my head held high and my girl by my side.

Thoughts of Quinn running out minutes ago dampen my enthusiasm, but it'll be fine, right? She's here. Shelly said she refused to leave. She'll come back to London with me. Right?

I hate that I'm feeling so insecure. Until this happened, I didn't once question whether Quinn was in this as deep as I was. Yeah, I knew she was scared, but she never let me see that she wasn't serious. She hasn't now, but with her being home and the two men who were haunting her gone, I just don't know what to think.

"Take a seat on there, young man," Shelly says, walking us towards a little white plastic seat. I couldn't be more grateful to get off my feet.

I moan in relief as the weight is taken off and I

relax back, so exhausted I could probably fall asleep right here.

"Okay?"

"Yeah. Do your worst."

"Lucky for you, I've got a gentle touch." She winks at me and I can't help but laugh. I regret it instantly, a sharp pain radiating from my wound and through my entire body. It's all forgotten though when she pulls my hospital gown from me and a warm torrent of water cascades over my shoulder and down my arm. It's fucking heaven.

"That temperature okay?"

"Incredible." I let my head fall back and focus on the feeling of the last few days washing away, forgetting that I'm stark bollock naked in front of a stranger. To be fair, I've been naked in worse situations.

It's over all too soon. Shelly helps me shave off some of the scruff covering my jaw, and when I eventually emerge, albeit slowly, from the bathroom, I feel like a new man. Well...one in more pain than he'd ever admit and who is about to pass out from exhaustion.

It's not until I stop at the bed that I realise we're not alone. Sitting in the chair, Quinn is waiting for me. My breath catches that she came back, and I really accept how afraid I was that she wasn't going to reappear. A lump clogs my throat and my eyes sting. It's not a feeling I'm very used to, but I'm so fucking relieved to see her.

"Quinn," I whisper, too exhausted to even say her name out loud.

"You look better." Her eyes hold mine as Shelly helps me back into bed.

"I'll leave you to get some rest. Buzz if you need anything."

"Thank you." She nods at me and disappears through the door, leaving me alone with my girl. "Come here." I'm surprised she hears me it's so quiet, but after a beat, she lifts herself from the chair and just about manages to climb onto the bed with me.

She rests her head down on the pillow next to mine and our eyes hold. I've not got the energy to tell her what I want to, so I just have to hope she can read it in my eyes.

I'm desperate to reach over and pull her body to me, closing the inch of space she's kept between us, but just as I think about moving my arm, my eyes fall closed and I'm lost to sleep once again. Who knew having a shower was such a fucking effort?

IT'S LATE when I come to once again. Quinn is back in her chair beside me, my entire body aching with the loss of her next to me.

She must feel my stare because her head lifts from the book she's reading and she graces me with a smile that makes my breath catch. It's the most genuine one I've seen since we returned from our trip to Stratford-upon-Avon.

"How are you feeling?"

"Lonely. Where'd you go?"

"Just here," she says with a laugh and shake of her head. "We haven't all been knocked out by surgery and pain killers."

"No but—"

"Not now, Joe. Not here." Her tone is harsh yet cold, and I can't help but agree. I'd also like to be somewhere a little more private to have that painful conversation.

"Good evening," a male nurse I've yet to meet sings, walking into the room with a tray full of hospital food. "I managed to work my magic and get you two a little extra."

"Thank you, Harry," Quinn says, wheeling my

little over-the-bed table thing for him to place it on. Clearly he's been here before.

His eyes linger on Quinn just that little bit too long, and my blood starts to boil. "How are you feeling now?"

"I'm fine," she replies unconvincingly. "It's him we need fixing."

"If you need anything, you know where I am."

"Thank you." The way she smiles at him makes me wonder if she knows him.

Harry drops the tray on the table and, after checking that I'm okay, leaves us to it.

"You know him." It's not a question.

"I do. I used to work with his mother. He was a student at Earlington, but that was long before I was teaching there."

"I see."

She sits forward on the edge of her seat, her eyes narrowing as they study my face. "Is that a little jealousy there, Mr. Kingsman?"

"What? No. I just thought he was a little overly friendly."

She chuckles. "Whatever you want to tell yourself. Shall we see what delights we have tonight?"

"Can't wait," I mutter. Knowing what the other meals have been like, I'm not all that excited.

I poke at the casserole looking thing in front of me, but all I can think about is the way that nurse looked at Quinn.

"I was jealous," I admit. "He looked at you like he knew you, and I hate that there are people out there who know you better than I do."

"Joe," she breathes, halting poking her own food around the container. "You are the only person who knows the true me. My real hopes and dreams. The version of me that lived here, that knew all these people, was a fake, an actress."

"Why didn't you get out sooner?"

She's silent for a few moments while she thinks. "I've been controlled my whole life. It was normal. It was expected of me to just do as I was told. It took me longer than it should have to realise that that control wasn't the love and care I thought it to be. I didn't know any different. The people my parents associated with were the same, but as I grew up and started getting a look at the world around me, I realised my life was anything but normal. By then it was too late. I'd been married off to one of my parents' friends' sons who'd lived the same sheltered and controlled life I had, only he thrived on continuing it. The longer it went on, the more I resented it, but I was in too deep to just walk away. They wouldn't allow that. I had to bide my time, continue to pretend to be her and just hope the time presented itself where I could live the life I'd been dreaming of."

My heart bleeds for her that she's been treated that badly for so long by people who are supposed to love and support her. I can sympathise to a point because my parents are worthless pieces of shit, but at least they didn't keep me locked up. Her story makes mine sound like a walk in the park. Yeah, I've had hard times, really hard, but at least I've always been able to be myself.

"I love the person you are." Her eyes fly to mine at my admission, but she doesn't say anything in response. I want to say more but when her eyes drop from mine in favour of the food in front of her, I get the message that she's done for now.

We finish eating in silence before Harry comes back and does my check-up before leaving us alone once again. There are a million and one questions on the tip of my tongue. I'm desperate to unleash all of them on her to fully understand everything she's been through, but in the end, I go with the most pressing.

"What happens when I get out of here?"

Her eyes meet mine and her lips part, ready to respond, but a knock on the door fills the room. She blows out a long breath. I'm not sure if it's because she's relieved or frustrated that she doesn't get to answer, but the second a head pops into the room all thoughts of my previous question leave my mind.

The woman who comes to stand at the end of my bed is so familiar. Okay, so her hair is blonde, but the blue eyes that are darting between the two of us are the exact blue ones I'm becoming used to.

"Mum." Quinn's voice is so quiet I almost miss it.

"Lizzie. I missed you so much." She walks towards Quinn with her arms open like she wants to pull her in for a hug, but Quinn stiffens, her tray remaining fully in place on her lap as if it's a shield. "Lizzie?"

"Don't," Quinn snaps in a tone I've not heard from her before. "You don't get to come in here after everything and act like all is well between us."

Pain fills her mother's face, and I can't help but feel for the woman. She's obviously gone out on a whim, hoping that her daughter might accept it. I can't really blame Quinn; from the little I know it seems to be that her mother, although not guilty of committing any of the crimes of the men in her life, must have been aware of them.

"Elizabeth, please, just let me explain."

"Explain? Explain how you sat back and allowed Dad and all the others to do what they did to those poor innocent kids? You could have done something about it long before I ever discovered it was happening, let alone before I worked at the same school. You could have—"

"I know," her mother sobs. "I know. But..." she pauses, looking up at the ceiling like she's praying for strength. "You know what your dad was like. You know how controlling he was. I just couldn't risk—"

"You couldn't risk what for all those children they were abusing on a weekly basis? What was so important to you that you couldn't help *them*? Help me? You knew the kind of monster you were marrying me off too. You could have stopped that."

"I just couldn't. I was scared."

"Scared? Scared of what?"

"Your dad," she whimpers. "He may have never laid a finger on you, but it was a very different story for me. If I made one wrong move I'd feel it for weeks. I couldn't risk exposing them and something happening to me. Where would that have left you? He might have...he m-m-might h-have touched you." Her sobs become uncontrollable, but Quinn doesn't move to comfort her.

I don't know the woman from Adam, but even from here I can tell that she's broken. Quinn might not want to hear her out, and that's fair after everything she's experienced, but I do believe there's truth in her mother's words. I've lived with manipulative parents who were only out for themselves, and I don't think this shell of a woman before me is one of them. Her father, on the other hand, is probably up there vying for king alongside my father and Lauren's. The reminder that all the women I care about have been screwed over by men who were meant to love and care for them has fury boiling in my veins. How hard is it to have a normal childhood with decent parents?

"Don't turn this on me. I was strong enough to deal with whatever was thrown my way. The fact we're all here right now should be proof of that."

"It is, baby. I'm so proud of you." Her face is red and blotchy and covered in tears and snot, her shoulders sagged in defeat, but still Quinn stands her ground.

"Why don't you think about all those kids whose endless abuse has hopefully come to an end, and all those adults out there whose lives will always be touched by what Dad did and allowed to happen under his leadership?"

"You think I've thought of anything else over the years?"

Quinn fumes but doesn't respond.

The silence is heavy with unsaid words. It's only her mother's lingering sobs that fill the space around us.

"Did you have anything else you needed to say?" Quinn's voice is cold and harsh. It's a million miles away from the soft woman I've fallen for, and I'm so damn hot for her right now. My cock swells beneath the sheets as she stands up against her mother, her eyes daring her to say something else.

I'm amazed that this strong woman before me endured everything she did for so long, but I do understand that bad situations aren't always the easiest to get out of.

"I just need you to know that I'm here for you, for whatever you decide to do next."

"Well, that's big of you, seeing as you've not cared since the day I walked out."

"Elizabeth, that's—"

"That's what? Not fair? How would it be, because you knew exactly where to find me. You were the only one who knew where I was going; I hoped that you'd have the strength to follow me, to find a better life for yourself as well, but just as I feared, you were too weak. You were too weak to stand up for what was right and too weak to give yourself the life you deserve."

"I couldn't. You've no idea what it was like after you left."

"Nor would you if you'd followed."

Her mother pales even further but nods in agreement. "You know where I am if you need *anything* when you both get out of here." Her eyes hold her daughter's a little longer before she turns to me. "I'm sorry we had to meet in these circumstances, but thank you for being there for my baby." She gives me a small smile before backing out of the room.

Having got a good idea of the life Quinn left behind and the fact that her mother turned up wearing a twinset and pearls, I was expecting judgemental eyes when she looked at me and found tattooed arms resting over the top of the sheets, or what's quite obviously not a posh boy face despite this morning's shave.

The sound of her footsteps fade, and, with a huge huff, Quinn falls back onto the chair and lifts her hands to cover her face, successfully cutting herself off from me.

It takes everything I have, but I swing my legs from the bed, ignoring the searing pain that shoots out from my belly. She's more important right now.

My legs feel a little unsteady as I push to stand, but they're not going to stop me. I shuffle towards her. She must know I'm coming, but that doesn't stop her flinching the second I wrap my hands around her wrists and pull her to stand before me.

Every muscle in her body is pulled tight, but she needs this. Gently, I close the space between us and wrap my arms around her. At no point does she relax in my hold, but eventually her trembling reduces.

"Everything's going to be okay. What you did was incredible." I want to tell her that I wish she'd told me, but I don't need her feeling any worse than she already is. I know that if she felt she could have told me, she would. I truly believe that if we had more time she would have opened up more, like she did in the church in Stratford-upon-Avon. She trusted me enough to begin her story. I have to believe that she would have trusted me with the rest.

"I promise I'll tell you everything," she whispers, "just not here, okay?"

I nod, my chin nuzzling against the top of her head as an idea forms in my mind. She wants to tell me everything but not here, and I don't want to be here.

We're forced apart when another knock sounds out, only this visitor is much more welcome than the last.

I release Quinn and scoop Lauren up in my arms. The fact that she made the trip up here for me means everything, especially after how selfish I've been, keeping this part of my life to myself.

She wraps her arms around me gently as I kiss the top of her head and breathe her in. She's always been my safe place, the rational head to my hot one, and I hate that since Ben came back into her life we've grown apart. There was a time not so long ago that I thought it would be Joe and Lauren forever, even if it wasn't romantically. But it seems life had other plans for us because she now has Ben and I've got Quinn...or Elizabeth. Jesus, this is such a fucking mess.

"Feeling better, I see," Lauren comments when

I release her.

"Like a new man," I lie. In reality I feel like shit, but if I'm going to convince them to go along with my plan, I can't allow them to see that. "So good, in fact, that I'm discharging myself."

"No you're fucking not," Lauren barks while Quinn stands, her hands going to her hips.

"You're staying exactly where you are until a doctor discharges you." Quinn's lips are pressed into a thin line, her blue eyes ice cold as she stares me down. She looks so cute being angry that I can't help but laugh.

"I'm fine." Summoning up every ounce of strength I have, I make a show of walking back towards my bed and pulling the cupboard open to get my clothes.

Pulling the items out, I find my jeans, boxers and shoes, but nothing to cover my top. I look up at Quinn, and she must sense where my thoughts are at.

"They had to cut them off you."

"I'm sure I rock the hospital gown anyway."

With both Lauren's and Quinn's concerned eyes on me, I pull my boxers on without groaning in agony and have my jeans halfway up when we're joined by Harry.

"Fantastic. Talk some sense into him. He thinks he's discharging himself."

Harry opens his mouth to do as he's told, but the second his eyes find mine, I think he appreciates that it's not an argument he's going to win.

"Obviously, my advice is that you stay as per doctor's orders, but—"

"See, it's fine. Even Harry thinks I should leave."

"Now, that's not exactly what I was getting at."

"Maybe not, but you also didn't tell me to get my arse back into bed. So, if you'd kindly remove this thing from the back of my hand, I'll be off."

Harry's chin drops as he looks between Quinn and me. I feel for the guy. He wants to do the right thing, but like fuck am I staying here any longer, getting poked and prodded and fed shitty food. It's time for me to take my girl for some alone time.

"I'm not happy about this," Quinn huffs as Harry does as he's told and removes the tube from the back of my hand.

"You'll need to be checked over by a doctor before you walk out, but I can get the paperwork for you."

"Thank you, I appreciate it."

He does his job and leaves as quickly as he entered.

"Why aren't you saying anything to try and stop this?" Quinn snaps at Lauren.

"Because there isn't a single thing I can say to him right now that will change his mind."

"This is bullshit."

"Your dumb arse decision aside, I was coming to let you know that I'm heading home. Ben and Erica need me back at work. I'm going to drive your van back and leave you two my car. Hopefully it'll be more comfortable for you to travel home in. That's assuming you're coming home." Lauren chews on her bottom lip as she waits for my response.

My eyes fly to Quinn, because she's the one to hold the answer to that question. Finding out where her head's at is part of the reason I'm getting the hell out of this place.

"He'll be coming home," she confirms, but in no way does she give me any clue as to whether she'll be coming with me or not. After watching her interaction with her mother earlier, I want to say that she has no intention of staying here, but I could be very wrong.

It wouldn't be the first time.

CHAPTER SIX

It took a hell of a lot longer than expected, but eventually the doctor begrudgingly allows me out of my little hospital room.

Quinn insists on finding me a wheelchair but like fuck am I leaving this place in a set of wheels. I'm walking out of this motherfucking building with my girl by my side and the world at our feet.

The reality of it is much more painful—and slower—than I was expecting, but eventually we make it down to reception and the electric doors slide open for us.

That first breath of fresh winter air is the best one I've ever had. The cold burns my lungs and the pain in my abdomen almost has me doubling over, but I fight it. It's going to take more than Quinn's psycho ex to break me.

"What car's Lauren got?"

"That white BMW," I nod to where it's parked and slowly Quinn helps me get across the road and to the passenger side of the car.

"For the record, I think this is a really bad idea."

It's not the first time she's expressed that, but just like all the times she's said the same thing, I ignore her and wait for the car to be unlocked so I can figure out a way to get inside.

Biting on the inside of my cheeks, I fold myself into the passenger seat, knowing that if I show even an ounce of how painful this is then she'll demand we go straight back inside.

I don't tell her where to go; I've got no idea where we are, but she doesn't ask, she just reverses out of the space and pulls out onto the main road.

"I'm assuming you've got a driving licence," I say with a laugh once the pain's subsided enough to be able to form words.

"Yes. I can legally drive, I'm even fully insured. You're in safe hands."

"I didn't doubt that for a second."

Silence falls around us. It's not uncomfortable,

but it's equally not really all that comfortable either. A million and one questions swirl around my head, but I know I need to wait. It's clear she has a destination in mind so I need to sit back and trust that she has a plan.

The motion of the car eventually forces me to put my head back, and, before I know it, my eyes have shut and I'm fast asleep once again.

I don't wake until I sense the car slowing to a stop.

"What's this place?"

"It's somewhere I've always wanted to stay. I thought this might be the perfect time to try it out."

"Looks expensive."

"You got your credit card on you?"

"Yeah, but—"

"This is on my husband. I think he owes us."

I think he owes us a little more than a fancy hotel stay, but I keep my mouth shut for now.

The second Quinn comes around to my door to help me out, I wonder how good a job I did at the hospital of looking like I wasn't in agony.

"I can see it in your eyes."

"What?"

"The pain. You're fooling no one, Mr.

Kingston, but I know better than to argue with you."

She leaves me on one of the giant sofas in the entrance while she books us a room. The hotel is stunning, but my eyes don't leave her for a second. I want to think this a good sign, that she hasn't sent me straight back to London alone but wants me to stay here—for a while at least.

She smiles the second she turns around and finds me staring at her. She still looks like she's been through the mill, but she's starting to resemble the Quinn I knew before. Her skin is brighter and her eyes are beginning to get their usual sparkle back.

"Come on, they've got the most incredible room for us."

I expect us to head towards the lift at the other side of the vast room, so I'm a little shocked when she walks us right past it and out of a huge set of doors.

We make our way down a path as the countryside opens up before us, revealing a huge lake surrounded by mountains.

"Whoa, this is kinda nice."

"Kinda nice? Is that what you city folk call the countryside?"

"Something like that. If this is a joke and you're expecting me to refuse to stay in a tent in favour of the hospital, then it's going to backfire on you. I'm not going back."

"I'm not expecting you to go back, or sleep in a tent. This is where we're staying."

She comes to a stop and waves her arm in the direction of a cosy little cabin with huge windows that overlooks the lake. The lighting on the inside looks warm and inviting, and I can see the flickering from a fire even from this distance.

"Just a slight upgrade from the hospital room."

"Come on." With her arm around my waist, we walk into the lodge together.

It's stunning, by far the most luxurious and expensive place I've ever stayed. If I knew this was where we were heading next, I'd have got myself out of that place even sooner.

"I'm pretty sure this is going to max out my credit card."

"I've got it covered, don't worry."

I stay quiet until she's got me settled in the chair in front of the fire. She steps away, but I catch her hand in mine, stopping her.

"Quinn?"

"Do you need anything? Are you hungry or..."

she trails off, sounding totally unsure of herself, and I hate it.

"I just need you." She releases a huge breath and turns to look at me. I hate the empty, haunted look in her eyes. I'd do anything to take all the terrible memories away.

"I'm here, Joe. I'm just..."

"I know, babe. Take as much time as you need. I'm here for you, don't forget that."

"Can I use your phone? I'm going to place some orders."

"Orders?"

"We've got no clothes. Toiletries. Anything. I've already spoken to a lawyer about a divorce—there's plenty of money that should come out of it. Well, if he agrees to it," she says sadly. "Financially, I'm okay. We can stay here as long as we need to, we can spend as much as we need to. You don't need to worry about that. Just...just get better, yeah?"

"It's just a little scratch."

Tears fill her eyes as I try to brush aside the seriousness of what happened. "I...I thought I was going to lose you. When I saw that knife go in...shit." A sob erupts, and when I pull her to sit on my lap, she doesn't deny me. She's been so strong while sitting beside me in hospital. She needs this.

I wrap my arms around her as she cries on my shoulder. Her tears continue for the longest time, but she can stay right here for a long as she likes. She's not the only one who had a fleeting fear that the other night might have been it for us.

Her sobs eventually fade, but she stays exactly where she is. "Babe?" I whisper, thinking she's fallen asleep. I don't expect her to move, but she pulls her head from my shoulder and looks up into my eyes. Her blue eyes hold so much within them. There's still fear, but there's also hope.

"Your eyes are really beautiful." She tries looking away, but I catch her cheek and bring her head back to me. "You really were hiding, weren't you?"

"It was stupid. He'd probably have recognised me from a mile away, but it made me feel better. I so desperately wanted to be someone else."

"Not at all. It was brave, Qu—what am I meant to be calling you?"

Her bottom lip trembles as she realises what I'm asking her. "Elizabeth is technically my first name, but I hate it. My dad chose it and I mostly despise everything he's ever touched. Quinn is my middle name. I didn't want to be a totally new person, so I went with that. I've always preferred it. It was my grandma's name."

"And what about Davenport, *Miss Smith?*" I give her a smile in the hope it shows her that I couldn't really give a fuck what her name is—it's the person she is that I've fallen for.

"Davenport is my married name. My maiden name is Montgomery. I used Smith because I thought it would help me blend in. Like I said, it was stupid."

"Quinn, you're anything but stupid. You're incredible. Everything you've done, everything you've been through. I'm blown away and I don't really know any of it." Guilt fills her face. "Don't give me that look. Take as much time as you need."

She nods but gently gets up. "Please can I use your phone?"

"Eat your heart out."

She takes my phone from my hand when I hold it out for her. I've no idea if it's got any battery or not; it's not exactly been my biggest concern the past few days.

She turns it on and then starts tapping at the screen. "Do you want to pick yourself some clothes?"

"Nah, you do it. I trust you." She smiles at me before looking back down. "I know one thing you can add though."

"Oh yeah?"

"One of those little nurse's outfits. You know the ones, nice and low, short, with some white stockings." I nod as the image of her wearing it appears in my mind. My cock swells and my heart rate increases as I imagine her giving me a one of a kind bed bath. *Oh yeah, maybe being a patient isn't so bad after all.*

The second I take in the panicked look on her face, all the images in my mind fade.

"What's wrong?"

"It's just...you wouldn't want that."

"You're joking, right? I want that more than anything." A smirk curls at the corner of my mouth, but it doesn't affect her.

"No, I'm not. You...you don't want that."

Faster than I can figure out how to respond, she's up and out of the chair and running towards the back of the lodge. A door slams shut, putting an end to our conversation and breaking the connection between us.

"Fuck," I mutter, rubbing my palm down my face. *What did I say that was so wrong?*

It takes longer than I'd like to get myself out of the low chair I'd all but fallen into, but eventually I'm following her tracks and come to a stop outside the door she disappeared behind. Her quiet sobs sound out and my heart breaks. My girl's much more affected by everything that happened than she's allowing me to see, and I hate that she's trying to deal with it all alone.

"Quinn?" I knock gently but there's no response. "Can I come in, babe?" Again, nothing but the sound of her cries.

I fucking hate this. I should be the one protecting her, drying her tears, not stuck on the wrong side of the fucking door. It was only a few days ago I smashed down a few to get to her—I won't bat an eyelid about having to do it again if necessary. Fuck the stitches in my stomach, I need her, damn it.

Taking a chance, I wrap my fingers around the handle and push. I'm amazed when it twists and the click of the latch moving fills my ears.

A knot of dread forms in my stomach at what I'm going to find on the other side. Ignoring it, I push the door open and step inside.

My breath catches when I find her sitting on the cold tiled floor beside the bath with her arms wrapped around her legs and her head resting on her knees. Her shoulders shake with her cries, and I want nothing more than to scoop her up into my arms and carry her to bed so I can hold her until she forgets. It kills me that I'm not able to do just that. Instead, I rest my back against the wall she's sitting in front of and slide down until my arse hits the floor beside her.

She stiffens when she realises I'm next to her. It's physically painful, but I just about manage to keep my hands to myself. I can practically feel the walls she's put up around herself, and I've got to respect that she needs some space right now.

The silence stretches out, and I start to think she's not going to say anything, let alone register that I'm sitting here with her.

"There was never any question that I would follow in my parents' footsteps and become a teacher. I never questioned it because as a child I idolised both of them. They were both intelligent, hard-working, and what I thought were the perfect parents.

"Dad was just a maths teacher when I was a kid. It wasn't until the year I left that he was promoted to head. Mum was only working part time by then, but she soon gave up. I assumed it was because they didn't need the money anymore, seeing as they'd moved into a school owned property. I was only to learn a few years later that my dad basically told my mum that she was done.

"I went to university, did my degree and my PGCE. My dad ensured I did my placements either at Earlington or at another local private school of his choice. I was still totally in the dark as to what he was really like. I assumed he just wanted the best experience for me to start my career off properly. I had no idea he was keeping me close, stopping me from seeing how different Earlington could be to other schools that would have alerted me to issues earlier on.

"It was a good school when I was there as a student. As far as I knew, the teachers enjoyed working there, the students were happy, and I never heard of anything untoward aside from the kids usual breaking of the rules.

"Dad ensured that I got a job with him. I didn't want to work there. I wanted to spread my wings. I also wanted to experience a state school to see what the differences would be. He told me that it would be hard work, that I'd regret it, a million and one excuses that I believed, and eventually I agreed and accepted the post he offered me as a newly qualified English teacher.

"That was probably his biggest mistake. He thought he could control me, make me believe that some of the accusations that started appearing were nothing more than lying, pissed off, privileged kids. He wanted me around to tell everyone else what an upstanding citizen he was and how trustworthy he was. But those accusations just kept coming. I could only defend him so many times before I started questioning him.

"By this time, Jeremy and I were already engaged. We'd been together a few years and friends, thanks to our fathers, since we were in nappies. It was almost expected that we'd end up together. I was naive. I thought he was cute. I thought he was caring in a similar way that my dad was. It was only years later that I'd discover that 'caring' was actually controlling. But it was all I'd ever known."

I blow out a slow breath as her words register within me. My fists clench as the level of passive-aggressive, controlling behaviour she's been subjected to her entire life becomes clear.

"Don't get me wrong, I loved—love—my job. It might have been expected of me but I truly can't imagine doing anything other than working with kids. But as the accusations started getting stronger, I started to resent everything.

"Jeremy and I got married and that was a serious turning point. Rumours started, accusations got more and more serious, and names started to be revealed. It seemed to be getting to the point that Dad couldn't sweep it all under the rug or pay off whoever it was who felt brave enough to poke their heads above the parapet.

"Somehow, no one ever went to the police. I assume because they didn't believe they'd win. My dad was an enigma, a power that no one thought they could touch. He controlled every inch of that school with a strength that appeared unbreakable."

"Until you broke him."

She nods, her hands trembling as she twists her fingers, lost in her memories.

"Jeremy's name started to be brought up and it coincided with him getting angrier and rougher with me at home. Since the day we got married he wasn't exactly pleasant to me, but he turned into a monster. I hated going home to discover what kind of mood he'd be in and what he thought I'd done wrong that day.

"He got the idea in his head that I should stop

teaching and be a housewife and mother to our kids." She laughs, but the sound is anything but joyful. "He was delusional. I was never going to allow him to bring another person into our fucked up world. It got the point that he assumed something was wrong with me because I couldn't fall pregnant. That only made his attitude and behaviour towards me even worse. I was pointless to him if I couldn't give him a son."

"Jesus," I mutter, trying to put myself in her shoes.

"I refused to give up my job. There was no way I was agreeing to basically have myself locked in that house like my mum was. I hardly ever saw her, and when I did it had to be meticulously arranged. She convinced me it was because she was busy with friends and bake sales for the church, but I soon discovered that was all a cover up. She was hiding. Hiding from my dad and his anger.

"I started digging into the accusations more. I'd talk to the kids, listen to all the rumours, but I wasn't getting anywhere. So I made a drastic move. I bugged Dad's office. Two days after I snuck in and hid the microphones, a fifteen-year-old boy accused Jeremy of sexually abusing him in his classroom.

"He was ignored, of course, brushed under the carpet like all the other indiscretions. Until I listened back to the recording from Dad's office. It got everything from Jeremy talking about the incident, as he called it, and Dad reassuring him that it could never be proved and he'd do whatever it took to keep his name clear.

"That Friday night, while they were all playing poker—if that's even what they actually did—I packed a small bag, said goodbye to my mum, took my recording to the police, and ran.

"Jeremy had kept me locked up to a point that I'd made no friends over the years, apart from one."

"Eddie," I add.

"I either went to him or...well, I didn't really have any other option. The streets, I guess. I left with only a bit of cash, leaving behind anything I thought could trace him to me. I dyed my hair, got new contacts that changed my eye colour, and I turned up at Eddie's door, hoping that our friendship was strong enough for him to help me. It had been two years since he'd got a job in London and left. He'd hated Earlington almost as much as I did. We connected immediately. By that point in my marriage, I was aware that Jeremy was doing his best to keep me locked up so I knew a friendship with another man was a sure fire way to set him off. We kept it on the down low for months before Jeremy made a surprise visit to my classroom one afternoon and found us laughing together.

"I could see the fire burning in his eyes and I knew I'd fucked up. That moment was where it really all changed for me. I knew I needed to find a way to get out. If me having a friend outside of our marriage was too much, then I knew it was time to end it. I just knew that wasn't going to be easy, and it was another two years before I found my way out.

"Thankfully, Eddie recognised me the second he opened his front door, and I guess the rest is history."

She falls silent. The words she just said to me hang heavy in the air between us. I've still got so much more that I want to know, but I keep my lips sealed. If I've learned anything about Quinn over the past few weeks, it's that she opens up when she's ready. I'll just have to wait for her, even if I want to shake her to find out the real reason she ran in here in the first place.

After dragging in a long, shaky breath, she

pulls her head from her arms and turns to look at me.

My breath catches at the exhaustion in her eyes. Reliving all that really just took it out of her. I'm just about to tell her that we need to go to bed when she beats me to it.

"You need sleep. You shouldn't be sitting down here on the hard floor with me."

Reaching out, I take her hand and lift it to my lips. The split is well healed after that arsehole punched me, but the roughness of the scab scratches against her soft skin as I kiss the back of her hand. "I'll sit anywhere you need me to."

Her eyes fill with tears once again, but she doesn't respond. Instead, she stands and reaches out to help me from the floor.

Getting up and to the bedroom is harder than I want to admit, and I'm in agony by the time Quinn's helped me drop my jeans and slip the damn hospital gown that I'm still wearing from around my shoulders.

I almost sigh when my skin connects with the soft cotton of the sheets after being stuck between scratchy hospital ones for the last few days, but I'm too exhausted now I'm down.

Quinn makes sure I'm comfortable before

pulling the sheets back and climbing in. She doesn't even attempt to undress; instead she lies beside me fully clothed, leaving too much space between us.

Rolling onto my side and breathing through the pain, I reach out and pull her into my body. She tenses the second I touch her, but she doesn't do anything else. I'm not awake long enough to know if she relaxes under my touch, and I fucking hate it.

CHAPTER SEVEN

Something drags me from my sleep and I lie awake for a few seconds before I realise what it was when Quinn flinches beside me again.

"No, no. Don't touch me."

My stomach turns over at what she must be reliving.

"Shhh...Quinn. It's okay. I'm here, you're safe." I gently stroke her cheek, the roughness of my thumb scratching lightly at her delicate skin.

Her head thrashes from side to side and I expect her to wake, but after a few more seconds, her breathing slows and she falls back to sleep.

Seeing the evidence of what she experienced first-hand is enough to have me wanting to go back and finish the job I started on that motherfucker.

There might not have been any charges after I assaulted him, but I'd happily take whatever I'd get if I were able to get my hands on him again.

When I wake again, the bed beside me is empty and the sheets are cold. The ball of dread that's still sitting heavy in my stomach after her admissions last night grows. She's not okay right now, but I'm at a total loss for what to do to help. Without knowing what happened, I don't even know what I'm dealing with.

The sound of water running fills my ears and I push myself up so I'm sitting. My need to go to her is too much to ignore, and before I know it I'm making my way towards the bathroom. I'm expecting the door to be locked, her way of keeping her distance, but I'm pleasantly surprised when I find it once again opens when I push the handle down.

Taking it as an invitation, I walk inside to find her.

Her back's to me as she stands under the waterfall shower. My eyes should be locked on where the torrent of water runs down over her back and onto her arse, but instead my muscles lock, my fists clench, and by some fucking miracle I manage not to growl like a feral fucking beast at the sight of the bruises that cover her body.

Blood rushes past my ears as my need to find that motherfucker and end him consumes me. I've no idea that I make a noise, but Quinn spins, her eyes wide as she tries to cover her body with her arms. But it's too late. I've already seen that that motherfucker's had his hands on what's mine.

The image of her running panicked in here last night hits me. She told me that I wouldn't want her in the sexy nurse's outfit I was joking about. This was why. The state of her body is why she tried to tell me that I wouldn't want her.

I've closed the distance between us before I've registered that my feet have moved.

"Joe?" Her brows draw together, her body trembling as I step up to her and under the water, still wearing my boxers.

It takes every single bit of self-control I possess to push down the images that are racing through my mind as to how he could have made these marks on her perfect skin as I lift my hand to her cheek and stare deep into her eyes.

The love I feel for her mixes with the raging inferno racing through my veins, and it allows me to focus on her, on the person who deserves everything I have, not the cunt who should be rotting in a cell for every single person he's hurt.

I drop my forehead to hers, our eye contact holding although hers is glassy with her unshed tears.

She wants to pull away from me and hide. Her body is locked up tight and she's trying to build her wall up so I can't climb over, but I won't allow it to happen.

"You never have to hide from me, babe. You're fucking beautiful."

A tear drops as she shakes her head so slightly that if we weren't touching I might miss it.

"H-He—" she sobs.

I take her face in my hands to stop her looking away from me. "He doesn't change how I feel about you. He doesn't stop this..." Taking her hand, I place it over my heart so she can feel it racing beneath my chest.

Her breath catches but she relaxes slightly, and I breathe a sigh of relief.

"Whatever happened, whatever comes next, we'll deal with it together. I'm in love with you, Quinn, and nothing about your past, no matter how recent, is going to change that. I promise."

Another sob erupts from her throat and I pull

her body into mine. She winces as I wrap my arms around her and hold tight, and I suck in a breath as she presses against my wound. We're both in pain, both broken, but neither of us attempts to move as the hot water cascades over us.

I've no idea how much time passes and, quite frankly, while she's in my arms I couldn't give a fuck. I've needed this since before I first opened my eyes and knew she was sitting beside my bed. Knowing she'd been taken from my arms inside that bedroom and having no idea what had happened to her was the worst thing I've ever experienced. Yes, her body is showing the evidence of her ordeal, but that'll fade soon. The wounds on the inside might take a little longer to lessen, but I'll do everything in my power to make it more bearable for her.

Eventually, Quinn moves her head. She twists slightly and reaches up on her tiptoes so she can drop a kiss to my neck.

A shudder runs through me before she lifts higher, her breath tickling my ears. Goosebumps prick my skin as I wait for her to say something.

"I keep remembering how his hands felt on my body." My heart thunders at her admission, and my hold on her tightens. "How badly I wanted to pull my own skin off to make it stop, to make all of it stop." She pauses, and I wonder if she has a point or is just trying to tell me what happened, but then she makes a request she knows I'd never be able to deny. "Take it away. Make me forget. Replace it with your touch."

"Fuck."

Dropping my hands to her hips, I force her to take a step back. My eyes skim down her body, taking in her curves and the angry welts and bruises that cover them.

My teeth grind to the point I fear I might break one at seeing the evidence of his abuse so clearly in front of me. Listening to what kind of a monster he was, the hints of things he might have done to her in the past was one thing, but this... The kind of anger this drags up is like nothing I've experienced before. I've hated my life and those around me with a passion but never to quite the level I feel for *him*.

"Joe?" Her voice is a soft plea as her fingertips brush my chest. It brings me back to what she's asked of me.

Taking a small step towards her, I lift her hand and bring her wrist to my lips. I kiss the delicate bruised skin that's been marred by the constraints he tied her with.

Her body trembles as I kiss all the way around, but she doesn't once try to pull her arm back.

My eyes find hers. If I'm going to continue, I need to know she's with me.

Her eyes hold fear, more than I ever wish to see within them again, but the blue I'm still so unfamiliar with also holds fire. My girl wants to fight, and I couldn't be prouder of her, knowing that she's taking control of what she needs to rid herself of him, of the past, of her memories.

I trail a line up her arm, kissing and licking at her sweet skin as I go. Goosebumps erupt the higher I get, and the fire in her eyes begins to win out over the fear.

I nip across one collarbone and then the other, her body trembling beneath my lips, but it's with need, not fear.

Sliding my fingers into her hair, I tilt her head back to give me the access I need to her neck as I make my way up to her lips.

"Joe," she moans as I suck on the sensitive skin beneath her ear. Hearing my name falling from her lips is like fuel to the fire that's already raging inside me. My need for her is all-consuming, but this isn't about me right now.

I kiss across her jaw before my lips find hers. As I suck her bottom one into my mouth, her eyes flutter shut.

"Look at me, babe. Let me see your beautiful eyes." Guilt fills them as she realises what I mean, but that wasn't why I said it. I thought she was stunning with her dark eyes; I hadn't been prepared for what these big blue ones would do to me, but one look into them and I'm on my fucking knees for this woman. I'd give her the fucking world if I could.

Not allowing her to dwell on her choices, I slam my lips down to hers and plunge my tongue into her mouth. She wastes no time in allowing hers to join and soon she's sucking it deeper. My cock throbs painfully behind the wet fabric of my boxers, wishing like hell it was that that was being sucked on.

My chest burns for air and I'm forced to pull back. Her breaths race out over my face and a smile twitches at my lips that I'm able to make her breathless from one kiss alone.

"Ready for more?"

She nods, her teeth sinking into her bottom lip,

but the second I pinch her nipples between my thumbs and forefingers, her chin drops and her gasp of shock sounds out over the running water. I love how responsive she is to my touch. I'm pretty sure I'll remember the night in the club when I'm on my deathbed. Feeling her coming apart beneath me while we were surrounded by all those people from my simple touch alone was hands down the hottest experience of my life. My need for her after that was off the charts, but she wasn't one of my usual hook-ups. I knew that the minute I laid eyes on her, and I was going to do everything in my power to do things the right way.

Her head falls back as I continue to tease and pinch her sensitive peaks. Her hips writhe as she tries to find some friction, and I can't hold back any longer.

Dropping to my knees, I ignore the pain radiating from my surgery and focus everything on Quinn and giving her exactly what she needs.

My eyes run over the marks he left on her stomach before they drop to her thighs. What I find has my movements halting and something wild exploding inside me. Pushing her legs wider, I find the rest of his handprints that are bruised into the soft skin of her inner thighs.

Everything around me fades as I stare at those marks. Images play out in my head of her lying on that cold, hard wooden floor as he...as he...

"Fuck," I roar, unable to keep a lid on my emotions. My hands tremble, my stomach twists, and my head spins as I sit there under the torrent of water, staring at what he did to my girl. *My* girl. I'm the only one who should be touching her. I should be the only one able to be in this position. "Quinn?" I ask, my voice weak and shaky as I try to prepare to hear the words I know that are to come. "D-did he..." I trail off, not even able to ask the question.

I can feel her stare burning into my top of my head as I focus on his fingerprints.

"Quinn, I need to know if—" My words are cut off when her fingers twist into my wet hair. She tugs slightly and I'm powerless but to look up at her.

Her eyes are full of unshed tears, her face pale and terrified. It's all I need for her to confirm my worst suspicions. She swallows, the muscles in her neck quivering with her uncertainty. She thinks I'm about to back away. She thinks I can't handle this. But everything I said to her earlier was true. Nothing about him or what happened will change how I feel about her. It won't change us. I refuse to allow it to.

She opens her mouth to say something. Knowing her, it's probably to apologise for something she had no fucking control over. Before a word passes her lips, I force her legs wider, part her, and lick up the length of her pussy.

If she needs to forget, then I'll damn well give her everything she fucking needs.

"Joe," she cries, but I don't react other than to up my tempo. Her fingers tighten in my hair and the pain is a welcome relief to the insistent one in my abdomen that won't abate.

"Oh god." Her hips flex, allowing me more access, and I thrust my tongue inside her as her legs tremble with the strength it takes her to stay upright.

She needs a distraction? Fuck if I'm not going to give her one.

I replace my tongue with two fingers and thrust them deep inside her, bending them so I know they'll hit the exact spot she needs. Her cries and mewls for more get louder and louder, encouraging me to push her higher.

Her body twitches and pulsates with the impending release, but I don't let her fall, not yet. I slow the pace, circle her clit with the tip of my tongue, and her entrance with my fingertip as she pants and demands more.

"You want more?" I ask, my voice deep and husky, showing my own hunger for her.

"More. Everything. Please, Joe, please."

Sliding two fingers back inside her, I lift my other hand and begin teasing her arse. She tenses for the briefest of seconds. I've no idea if this is what she had in mind when she said everything, but I trust her to tell me to stop if she doesn't want it.

But she never does. The water running down her back is enough to allow me to push my finger inside her, and she howls with pleasure as I stretch her open.

She's unbelievably tight, her muscles clamping down on my finger as my cock weeps to feel that kind of pressure. I suck her clit into my mouth, grazing it with my teeth, and with her full of me, her hips buck violently as she screams out my name, her pleasure racing through her body, making her legs go weak. Her fingers grip once more as she tries to stay upright as she rides out the pleasure.

Watching her come apart above me, even as

broken as she is right now, is one of the most beautiful things I've ever seen. My heart damn near burst out of my chest for this incredible, brave woman before me.

Once she's ridden out every wave of pleasure, I pull my fingers from her and sit back on my heels. My cock's trying to rip through my boxers as I watch her chest heave as she tries to catch her breath.

Without thinking, I press my hand to my side, where the dressing is coming undone with the amount of water that's soaking into it.

"Shit, you shouldn't be getting that wet."

"I don't give a fuck. You needed me. I'm here." I climb to my feet and take her face in my hands. I want to say it's smooth, but the reality is anything but.

"But—"

"No buts."

"Okay, but I really think you should go and lie down." I want to argue and tell her that I'm fine, but I think we'd both know that would be a lie. "I'll order us some breakfast and we can see what's on the TV." It's her way of putting off the conversation from last night that we need to continue. Although our impromptu shower has answered quite a few questions I had about what happened while she was locked up in that bedroom, I won't be happy guessing based on her injuries. I need her to tell me. At least that way it'll stop my imagination going wild.

With Quinn's help, I drop my sopping wet boxers to the tiled floor and wrap a fluffy white towel around my waist. I want to stay and make sure she's okay after everything that just happened, but I'm struggling to hold myself upright.

Using the wall for support, I make my way to the living room and lie back on the sofa to the sounds of her faffing around in the bathroom.

Ignoring the TV for now, I focus on the scenery outside. I love London; it's the only home I've ever known, but I can't imagine wanting to move there after living somewhere as beautiful as here. I always thought I'd be a Londoner forever, but just my short time here is giving me ideas about my future that have never been there before. Suddenly I'm seeing a life in a house in the country with Quinn and a couple of kids. My heart races, but it's not with the panic I thought it would be with the images that are playing out so clearly in my mind.

I've always said point blank that I've never

wanted to settle down. Never wanted to have kids and subject them to even an element of what I've had to suffer during my life, but suddenly none of that matters because I know that, with Quinn by my side, I'd never need to worry about our children suffering because they'd have the most incredibly supportive mother. We've both been screwed over by bad parents, and I can't help but wonder as I lie here with the winter sun streaming in through the huge windows if all of that bullshit was just preparing us for our future as parents ourselves. We've both experienced how bad it can be; we know exactly what not to do.

"What's put that smile on your face? I thought you'd be frustrated with blue balls," she says with a laugh. My heart drops slightly when I see she's totally covered up again in those damn leggings and what I've realised is Lauren's hoodie.

"Just thinking about our future," I admit.

"Our future, huh?" She comes to sit on the free bit of sofa beside me and places her hand on my chest.

"Yep. Wondering what our kids might look like."

Her eyes widen in shock, but she doesn't look totally opposed to the idea. "You're not serious?"

"Deadly. I thought I'd lost you, Quinn. When I turned up to class and found Eddie standing at the front of your classroom, I thought that was it for us."

"I'm sorry." She looks away as if she's ashamed of everything that's happened.

"Hey, don't do that." Lifting my hand, I cup her cheek and turn her back towards me. "Don't apologise for anything you didn't have control over. The only thing I wish was different is that you'd told me what kind of danger you were in. I'd have done anything in my power to protect you."

"I didn't want to drag you into all this."

"How'd that work out for you?" Her eyes fill with tears.

"You're not the only one who thought they'd lost something. I'll never forget that moment as I watched him slide that blade into your stomach."

"I'm fine."

"Just—"

"Ah, come on, babe. It'll take more than a little knife wound to kill me off."

"Little? You saw the size of that thing, right?" Of course I had, I was the one who grabbed it from the kitchen to free her from her restraints. "I need to change this dressing," she says. Clearly her previous question was rhetorical.

She's up off the sofa and at the other side of the room, rummaging through the bag of stuff we left the hospital with, before I have a chance to blink.

She lines everything up on the coffee table in front of us before turning back to me, ready to start picking off the wet bandage that's still attached to my stomach. She starts scratching at the corner, trying to lift the sticky stuff, but it hardly budges now it's dried.

When she does eventually manage to get enough up to grab, she pulls it and I cry out.

She damn near jumps a mile, her wide, panicked eyes turning to me. She's totally horrified that she hurt me.

"Shit, I'm sorry. I was trying to be gentle."

I try to stop my lips twitching, but I lose the fight and a wide smile tugs at my mouth.

"You little shit." She swats my shoulder gently as she realises that I'm having her on. Okay, it hurt a little where it caught my hair, but it wasn't a pain worth crying about. Who am I kidding? She's got her hands on my bare skin. I'm not going to do anything to put an end to that.

She goes back to the task at hand and gently

pulls the bandage from my skin. I'm fascinated by the sight of her delicate fingers touching me so softly.

"It looks like it's healing well."

"Good." I don't look at my wound. Instead my eyes lift to her as she works. Her dark, wet hair is falling like a curtain around her face as she studies my stomach. Every time her skin connects with mine, my muscles twitch, but at no point does it distract from how beautiful she is.

My cock stirs once again behind the towel, and she doesn't miss it. Her eyes drop lower and a small smile curls at her lips.

"I'm pretty sure you should be focusing all your efforts on getting better," she whispers.

"Not possible when you're touching me."

"Even after—"

My fingers circle her wrists, stopping any more movement and cutting off her words.

"I meant what I said. I'm in love with you, Quinn. What you went through and what he did doesn't affect that. I want to kill that motherfucker with my bare hands for ever thinking it's okay to lay a finger on you, but it'll never stop me wanting you."

Her eyes hold mine. It's as if she's waiting for

me to tell her that I'm lying, but she's going to be waiting a long time if that's the case. My heart pounds against my ribs as I wait for her to do something, my cock pressing against the towel, hoping to get some action.

"You need to rest."

Tugging on her wrist, I pull her so she's hovering over me. "What I need is you." Her eyes bounce between mine as she tries to figure out what to do for the best.

"If it hurts, at all, tell me and I'll stop." Her face is totally serious, and I find myself agreeing even though I already know that once she touches me, nothing will make me stop her.

She finishes reapplying my fresh bandage before dropping her lips to my abs. She kisses along the indentations until she finds the top of the towel. My eyes follow her every movement, my body desperate for her to unwrap the fabric and touch me after being away from her for so long.

My fingers dig into the sofa as I attempt to fight my need to flip her over and fuck her six ways from Sunday. I need to give her the space to do this at her own pace. I've no real idea where her head's at right now. I don't want her to feel like I'm pushing her into anything.

She glances up, wraps her fingers around the fabric at my waist, and smiles. It's wicked and full of promises, and excitement explodes in my belly. After everything, my Quinn's still in there somewhere. I can't deny that it's not a relief to see that little sparkle in her eyes.

Slowly, painfully fucking slowly, she pulls the towel from around my waist and allows it to fall to the sofa. Her eyes burn a trail down my torso before she finds my cock. She bites down on her bottom lip as she watches it twitch with need.

I wait. It's hard as fuck—pun intended—but I'll wait forever if I have to.

Her eyes flick to mine, but unlike what I'm expecting, there's no hesitation in them. Finally, she reaches for me and wraps her slender fingers around my solid length. My hips buck from the sofa and I groan. It's a mixture of delight and pain, but thankfully from the way her eyes shine with achievement, she only hears the lust.

"Fuck, Quinn," I moan as she slowly moves her hand up and down. I've not come since we were in Stratford. I was fucking desperate after we were interrupted by Erica, but I told myself that the next time I got off, it would be at her hands because I was determined to ensure that things were far from over between us—whatever it took—when I saw her again. I just never could have imagined the situation that was about to unfold.

"So fucking good."

She leans forward and licks the tip of my cock. I damn near come on the spot.

"Jesus."

Running her tongue around the top, she then lowers her mouth down my length. Threading my fingers into her hair, I help to guide her. My balls draw up all too soon and tingles erupt in the base of my spine.

"Quinn, I'm gonna—" I don't get a chance to finish my warning because she takes me right to the back of her throat and I explode.

My chest heaves, my body tingling with the aftershocks of my release, but as it begins to fade, the pain begins to make itself known once again.

My hand moves to rest on top of my fresh bandage. Quinn follows its movement and the blood drains from her face.

"Shit, did I hurt you?"

"It was so worth it."

"Fuck." She jumps up from her spot perched on the edge of the sofa and backs away like being close to me might be causing me pain. "Have you had your meds yet?"

"No. How about I take them, we wait an hour, and we can crack on with round two?" I lift a brow in the hope she agrees, but when hers pull together I know it's not going to happen. Shame, I could really do with being inside her right about now.

She rushes over to the bag she got the bandage from and pops out the pills I need before bringing them over with a fresh glass of water.

"What do you fancy for breakfast?" I open my mouth to respond, but I don't get a chance to say anything. "Don't say me. It's not happening. Not until you're healed."

"Spoil sport." I sulk.

CHAPTER EIGHT

We end up staying in our little lodge for five days before Quinn decides I'm allowed out into the world again. As much as I'd like to re-join real life, I'm also a little sad to leave our haven behind... although I'm hoping that getting back to London and putting some distance between Quinn and this place might help with her nightmares that seem to haunt her each night. I'd do anything to take away her pain, her memories, but I'm powerless to do anything but hold her as she cries. It's been incredible just being the two of us, finding out all the little things about each other that we'd not had a chance to do until this point.

Quinn opened up more about her previous life. Although she was understandably reluctant to tell me some of the darker parts, she managed it. I think she was worried about my opinion, but after telling her for the millionth time that the stuff that's happened in the past doesn't bother me, I think she's starting to believe me.

She makes me sit on the edge of the bed while she packs up the small amount of stuff we have. Seeing as she was brought here against her will and I arrived in a bit of a panic, all we have is what Quinn ordered for us when we first got here.

Thankfully, her bruises have almost completely faded now. I can see her confidence come back a little more each day, and it's incredible to witness. She's becoming the Quinn I fell for again and somehow managing to put *him* behind her.

"I can help, you know. I'm not completely useless."

"Just chill out. We've got a long journey."

"We're going to London, not Australia. I'll be fine."

"You say that now; you've not experienced my motorway driving."

I laugh at her but stay put as she carries the bags to the front door.

"I'm not sure I'm ready to leave this place in favour of that damp studio flat in London."

Stepping up behind her, I wrap my arm around her waist, drop my head to her neck and breathe her in.

"Move in with me?"

She tenses but doesn't immediately say no. "Don't you live in your friend's flat? I can't imagine she wants me there." Her voice is flat, and it gives me a little hope that she might actually be up for this.

"I've actually moved into her boyfriend's place upstairs so they can be together and there are no more accidental interruptions. Trey said I can stay there as long as I'd like, but if you're up for it, I'd really love to get a place of our own sometime soon."

Turning in my arms, she looks up at me, an unreadable expression on her face. "You're serious, aren't you?"

"Deadly. I don't want our time together to be over."

"But I'll be there every day. It won't be like it's been here. We'll have to work and—"

"I'm aware that I'm not asking you on a long-term holiday, Quinn. I know we're going to have responsibilities and that at times, it's going to be stressful. I've never done it before, but I want it all with you. I want the nights cuddled on the sofa, the lazy Sunday mornings. I want the heated arguments and the hot make-up sex afterwards. I want a future, Quinn, and that's something I'd never thought I'd say."

She's silent for a beat too long, and I almost find myself telling her to forget about it and attempting to convince her that it was a joke, but then she opens her mouth and just one quiet word leaves her lips that makes every part of my life fall into place.

"Yes."

"Yes...as in yes you'll move in with me?"

"Yes." A smile twitches at the corners of her lips as my heart races. "Yes, I'll live with you." It's much louder this time, almost a squeal before she wraps her arms around me and holds as tight as she can without hurting me. "I love you too." She mumbles it against my chest so quietly I almost think I've misheard her.

Pushing against her shoulders, I force her to move back a little.

"What was that?"

When her eyes find mine, they're full of

unshed tears and swimming with emotion. "I love you too, Joe."

My fingers twist in her hair and I pull her lips to mine. My heart damn near beats out of my chest as I repeat those three little words in my head. I've heard them before. Lauren says she loves me, Erica's even said it once or twice, but I've never heard it in this way, and fuck if it's not just knocked my world upside fucking down.

My cock swells against her stomach, still desperate for some real action, but sadly she takes a step back, putting some space between us.

Her chest's heaving just as much as mine as we stand there silently for a few moments, absorbing what just happened between us.

"Before we do this, there's something I need to do. You're welcome to come or you can just wait for me. It's up to you."

She looks unsure of herself and I hate it. Reaching out, I take her hand in mine. "I'll follow you anywhere, Quinn."

"I thought you might say that. Come on then, the sooner we get this over with the sooner we can head home."

Home. I've called a few places home in my life, but I can honestly say that this is the first time I feel like I really have one. It doesn't matter that the flat we're going back to is someone else's; all that matters is that she's going to be by my side.

We load Lauren's car, but the second Quinn puts an address into the SatNav I know exactly where she's going.

I stay quiet as she drives the relatively short journey back to her old house.

"I always hated this house," she murmurs as she pulls the car to a stop in the driveway beside the two cars still parked out the front. "It's cold. Unwelcoming. Kind of fitting, I guess."

"Do you own it?"

"No, it's a school property. Dad ensured we got the best one—well besides his."

"It's a nice house."

"Is it?"

I don't respond. She doesn't need me to.

Eventually she climbs from the car and I follow her towards the front door.

There's a little key lock that she quickly opens to reveal a key. She sucks in a large breath before lifting it to the lock. Stepping up closer behind her, I press my hand into the small of her back in support and she unlocks the door.

We step inside in silence and I follow her as

she pokes her head into every room. I've no idea if she's come here because she needs to get stuff or what, but she can have all the time she needs.

I didn't pay any attention to the interior of this place the last time I was here aside from the dark room Quinn had been locked up in, but it's exactly as I'd have imagined from everything she's told me about her previous life. Everything is just so. It's all clearly expensive and has its place. It reminds me of my parents' house, and I hate it.

I follow behind her, taking everything in and fighting the memories from my childhood that keep threatening to pop up. Nothing I ever did in that house was good enough. I was always made to feel like a failure and a disappointment—two things I'd quite happily never feel again.

"Joe, are you okay?" Quinn asks, turning and coming a stop in front of me. She reaches out and takes both my hands in hers.

"Of course, why wouldn't I be? I should be the one asking you that question. Being back here must be—" I trail off, not really knowing the right word to use.

"It's...closure. This part of my life is over. But you look like you're about to throw up."

"I'm fine." She eyes me curiously, but,

obviously not wanting to spend any more time here than necessary, she doesn't question me.

Before she takes a step up onto the stairs, she sucks in a huge breath.

"You don't have to do this."

"I do." Squaring her shoulders, she begins to climb and I keep right behind her.

Ignoring most of the doors, she stops at one and pushes it open.

The room is an office, much like the one I saw through the window at the school, with a huge mahogany desk and leather chair sitting behind. It's nothing but pretentious. I can't imagine for a second that Quinn ever worked in here.

She walks behind the desk and takes a seat before looking up at me. "Can you get into this?"

Not knowing what she means, I follow her lead until I'm staring at the same drawers she is.

"It's locked," she adds, just in case I hadn't already figured that out.

"So you think I'm capable of breaking and entering?" I raise an eyebrow at her in accusation.

"How did you get in here to find me in the first place?"

"I smashed your back doors in."

"Case in point. Now..." She waves her hand in front of the somewhat flimsy drawers and waits.

"You got a crowbar or something?"

"What, no lock picking?"

"Nah, I missed that day at school."

"Under the stairs there should be a tool box. See what you can find."

I follow her instructions and am soon standing with my head in the understairs cupboard, rooting through a huge bag.

Crowbar in hand, I head back to find her. She's still behind the desk, but she's now got the computer on and is furiously writing stuff down into a notebook.

The floorboards creak as I step into the room. Her head flies up and panic fills her eyes for the briefest moment, showing me that she's anything but fine being here, but that fear soon morphs into something else. I've seen that hungry look on her face once before. It was the day I unexpectedly picked her up from work and was covered in a day's worth of dirt. I expected her to be disgusted, she didn't seem like a girl who'd be willing to sit inside a dirty work van, but the girl I actually picked up that day was far from what I imagined.

Her eyes darken as she stares at me with the

crowbar bouncing in my hand before they drop to my body. I'm wearing a plain black t-shirt and a pair of grey joggers, but the way she's feasting on my body, you'd think I was naked. My cock swells as images of what I'd like to do to her in the place she lived with her cunt of a husband fill my mind.

Taking a step forward, and then another, I delight in watching her chest begin to rise and fall faster.

"Do you have any idea how badly I want to fuck you over your husband's desk right now?"

Her pupils dilate, the blue damn near vanishing as her cheeks heat and she squirms in the seat. It's all I need to know that she's as up for this as I am.

Sadly, when she opens her mouth, she doesn't say what I'm hoping for.

"And do you know how badly I don't want you back in the hospital because you've split your stitches? There will be no desk fucking until you're healed."

"Jesus." I lift my hand to my hair, tugging on the length as I repeat those two words in my mind. *Desk fucking.* Her voice sounds so soft and innocent as she says them, but I know for a fact that she's imagining it just as much as I am right now.

Stalking towards her, she wheels the chair back slightly but doesn't really want to escape. I can see the delight in her eyes as my hands land on the arms, caging her in.

"You do like to pretend to be a good little girl, don't you?"

"I just...d-don't...fuck." Her words falter when I slip my hand up the inside of her hoodie and t-shirt to find her bare breast beneath. Her nipple pebbles against my touch instantly, making my already growing cock solid with my need for her.

"Joe...we...we can't," she moans, the breathy sound to her voice at odds with her words.

"Says who? Your ex-husband? Fuck him. He gave up any right to an opinion the first time he mistreated you."

"Joe, we can't."

"Shhh." Wrapping my hands around her waist, I lift her from the chair and deposit her on the edge of the desk. My stomach pulls, telling me that she's right about the fucking, but that doesn't stop me giving her one final memory of this place in an attempt to erase a few of the old ones.

Gripping onto the waistband of her leggings,

she lifts her hips and allows me to slip them from her body. I discard them in a pile on the floor before dropping to my knees and spreading her legs as wide as they'll go.

She stares down at me as I focus on her centre. "Let's show him how it should have been done," I mutter before leaning forward and licking up the length of her. Her legs tremble under my palms and a moan of pleasure rips from her lips.

"Fuck yes."

She watches me the entire time, and my chest swells with the knowledge that this moment is one she wants to remember from this house. Knowing that I might be able to take even a tiny bit of the horror away that went on under this roof is everything to me.

As I slip two fingers inside her, her muscles clamp down, making me wish it was my cock. I'm fucking desperate for her, but I also don't want to end up back on a hospital bed being stitched up.

My fingers curl, hitting her sweet spot, and she cries my name out into the otherwise silent house. Two more licks to her clit and she's falling, pushing out all the old nightmares and allowing this sweet memory to replace them.

I lick at her until she's come back down from

her high. Her chest heaves, her cheeks and neck flushed with her pleasure. It's a sight to fucking behold, and it's all fucking mine.

Sitting back on my haunches, I watch as she drags in some much needed air, her legs still apart, giving me the best view of my life.

"Well...I can safely say that's never happened here before."

"Sex in the office?"

"I was more thinking of me getting a happy ending."

"Wait...he never...?" I trail off, too stunned to finish the question.

"Nope. Never."

"I know he's done some seriously unforgivable shit but not even allowing you that pleasure is up there with the worst of it."

"I'm not sure if it was a case of him not allowing it or him unable to."

"Really?" My male ego swells at her statement. "So am I the only one to—"

"Give me an orgasm? Besides myself, yeah. What?" she asks when I don't say anything.

"Just imagining what that might be like. I think you might need to show me exactly how you do it one day."

She swats my shoulder as she stands and rights her clothing. "Let's get this shit done and get out of here, yeah?"

"Whatever you say. Take whatever time you need." I fall back onto the arsehole's chair. My raging hard-on is obvious beneath the fabric of my trousers. Quinn's gaze falls to it and conflict fills her eyes. "Just do your thing. That'll wait." It pains me to say it, but it's the truth. It'll still be hard once we're back and away from this hellhole.

"I need these open." She points to the drawers we came in here for in the first place, and I'm reminded that she sent me on a mission before I had her legs spread on the desk.

"My pleasure."

It takes mere seconds for the old wood to splinter around the flimsy locks. The drawers slide open, mostly revealing a load of crap, but when she pulls the bottom one out I soon understand why she wanted it all. She pulls out paperwork for multiple bank accounts, her passport and driving licence along with her birth certificate.

"I couldn't get in here for all this before I left. He kept this room secured like Fort Knox."

Her words fade off as I notice one of the figures on the bank statements. "Jesus, Quinn. This all yours?" I don't think I've ever seen so many digits on a bank account before.

"It's a joint account but yeah, that's mine."

"Fucking hell, no wonder you weren't worried about bending my credit card on that luxury lodge."

"The lawyer I've been talking to says that I could probably take him for everything after what he's done."

"No less than you deserve."

"Maybe. I'm not sure I can leave him with nothing, though. He might be a monster, but he has worked for this."

"Fucking hell, Quinn. You're more forgiving than me." She shrugs as she finishes off finding what we need.

"With a bit of luck the divorce papers will be inside my flat when we get back and I can get the ball moving. The sooner I lose my surname the better."

I bite down on the inside of my cheeks so hard that the metallic taste of blood fills my mouth as I attempt to keep the words, 'you can have mine instead' inside.

"You think he'll make it easy on you?"

Her sad laugh says it all, but she backs it up with, "We can only hope, right?"

She finishes collecting everything she needs before we walk out of the room. She looks down at where the door is still swinging in the wind from where I smashed it down, but she makes no move to go down that end of the hallway. I can't say I blame her; her memories must be enough.

"That was my office. It was all cream and gold. I used to love it in there."

I remember the black walls and hard floorboards from when I found her. Clearly the douchebag did some decorating after Quinn left.

"Are you done?" I ask as we descend the stairs.

"Yeah. Let's get the hell out of here."

CHAPTER NINE

————————

It's just a simple car journey. It should be easy, but by the time I climb out of Lauren's car outside Quinn's building, I ache like a motherfucker.

Quinn wanted to stop, but I insisted I'd rather just get back so she drove us straight here. In hindsight it might have been a mistake, but at least we're back now. A quick trip up to her flat for some of her stuff and then home. Well...the flat Trey rents, but it's home for the two of us for now. I'm hoping we can start searching for our own place as soon as possible. I'm ready for it, ready for my future with this girl.

"Why are you smiling?" she asks, taking my hand as we walk towards the entrance to her building. The door is still fucked and just another reason why she shouldn't stay here, even if the threats are now behind bars.

"Just thinking about us...the future."

Her hand squeezes mine. "It's exciting, isn't it?"

"I understand it now—how Lauren couldn't refuse Ben when he came back into her life. How Erica couldn't deny Trey when he kept pushing. This thing. This connection. It's...unbelievable." Turning her into my chest, I tuck her hair behind her ears and stare into her eyes. The physical evidence of her ordeal is all but gone now. I'm relieved that she's not reminded of it every time she looks in the mirror. "It's everything. You're everything."

Her eyes fill with tears, but there's a smile on her face. "I don't even know how to thank you for everything you've done."

"No need, babe. I'd go to the end of the earth to find you. Now, come on, I can't wait to take you home."

"Okay," she whispers, excitement filling her voice. Her step is lighter as she turns back towards the building.

Quinn lets out a little squeal when she stops at the post boxes and finds a huge manila envelope with a lawyer's stamp on the front. Her excitement is infectious, and I find myself getting carried away with thoughts of making her mine once again.

"Now we wait to find out if he's going to sign his copy."

"You confident?" I ask as we climb the stairs.

She hesitates, but after a second she turns to me, a wide smile on her face, and says, "Of course. We're done. What's the point in refusing now?" I don't point out that her ex-husband is quite obviously a control freak and will probably want to manipulate her any chance he gets, even from behind bars.

We fill a couple of black bags with her few belongings and she finally gets the chance to put the old soup and very mouldy bread in the bin.

"It might sound odd," she says as we head back down the stairs, "but I think I'm going to miss this little flat."

"That's not odd."

"I'd dreamed about what this place might look like for years. The place that I'd escape to. My sanctuary away from my past. It might not have been much, but it's everything to me."

"Plus, it's where you were living when you found me."

"I'm pretty sure *you* found *me*. You were the one who walked into my classroom looking all bad boy nerd. I didn't stand a chance."

We've steered clear of talking about the whole student/teacher issue while we've been away, but as she says the word 'classroom' her voice drops and I'm reminded that we've got some hard conversations ahead of us. *She's moving in with me.* That's all the reminder I need to know that whatever comes next doesn't matter. I'll forget all about qualifications and a better job as long as I have her by my side. That's if Eddie would even let me back after everything.

I'm desperate to ask what she wants to do, but I keep my mouth shut until we're settled and less exhausted from the journey.

"Ready to go home?"

"So ready."

I direct her to my building and in no time we're pulling Lauren's car into my parking space out front.

By some fucking miracle, the out of order sign on the lift is nowhere to be seen. I breathe a sigh of relief that we don't have to carry the contents of the car up four flights of stairs to Trey's flat.

"Wow, this place is nice," Quinn says, walking

in ahead of me and placing the bags on one of the sofas.

"Yeah, I could have found myself in a worse place, that's for sure."

"You go sit down." I turn to her to argue, but she doesn't allow it. "I know you're struggling. Just go and sit down and I'll get the last of the things."

"No need," a very familiar voice says from the doorway. When I turn back I find both Erica and Trey with armfuls of our bags.

"Stalking much?" I ask with a laugh, assuming they heard our footsteps and ran to find us.

"I'm so glad you're okay." Erica's eyes are a little wet as she runs at me and wraps her arms around my waist.

It hurts, but I don't give a fuck. Returning her hug, I drop a kiss to the top of her head.

"Okay, enough of you. I need to meet your girl properly." She wipes the tears staining her cheeks that are probably courtesy of her pregnancy hormones.

Erica turns to Quinn and none of us miss the redness of her cheeks as she's reminded of the first time they met. Quinn might be embarrassed, but I know Erica better than that and she won't give a fuck about finding us mid-fuck. It won't faze her in the slightest.

She opens her arms and Trey and I watch as Erica pulls Quinn into her embrace. She says something in Quinn's ear that we're too far away to hear, but whatever it is has Quinn looking up at me over Erica's shoulder. Her eyes are soft and her smile is easy, and I relax for the first time since she walked away from me the morning she claimed to need space. I didn't realise it was still eating at me, but having her here, in the arms of one of my best friends, it really settles inside me that this could be it.

"We should leave you to get sorted," Erica says, releasing Quinn. "I just needed to see for myself that you were okay."

"Stay for dinner?" I ask without thinking. This living with someone and having to ask their opinion is going to take some time to get used to. It's just that now I'm surrounded by my people once again, I'm not ready for them to leave quite yet. My eyes fly to Quinn—I'm about to apologise when she nods.

"Yes, I'm starving. What about Lauren and Ben, should we ring them?"

There's a moment of silence as all eyes turn on

me. Quinn's just curious about inviting more of my friends while both Erica and Trey smile at me with knowing eyes. They've both realised just how far gone I am for this girl. She gets me. She knows that the only thing missing right now is my best friend and that, after everything we've just been through, I need this. I need my people, and I need to be normal. More than that, I need her to be part of my normal.

"I'm on it," Erica announces, pulling her phone out and turning away slightly.

I reach my hand out, and Quinn walks over and gently wraps her arms around my waist. "Thank you."

"I know how much you missed them. It's nice to see you smile like you did when they turned up."

"I smile more than I ever have with you."

"I know, and I love it. But they're your family. I get it."

"And what about yours?"

"My family? I don't have a lot of that these days." The sadness in her voice is like a physical pain to my chest. I want to talk to her about her mum but right now is not the time for that. Once the dust is settled, maybe I'll bring it up.

"I was thinking of Eddie. You want to invite him to join us?"

"Really?" Her brows draw together in confusion. "I didn't think you liked him."

I think for a moment to find the right words to describe my feelings for Eddie. Is he a judgemental prick? Yes. But he's helped Quinn out when she's needed it the most, and he had my back when we went after her. Kind of. But if he means something to Quinn, he's important to me. End of.

"I don't really know him, but I know you, and if you say he's a good guy, then I'll give him all the time in the world to try to prove it."

"Thank you."

"If it wasn't for him, I'd never have found you." A shudder runs up my spine as I wonder what might have happened had that been the case.

Quinn goes over to find her phone, which is dead after being abandoned in her flat for over two weeks.

"You want to use mine?" Taking it from my hand, she finds his number and lifts it to her ear. "You think he'll be able to cope with all the ink?" I nod over to Trey, although most of his is hidden beneath his shirt. Ben's, however, will be very much on display for Eddie to disapprove of.

"I'm hoping you might have smashed a few of his preconceived perceptions after saving my life."

I swallow down the emotion that statement drags up. Is that what I did? Would he have gone that far?

Seeing where my thoughts are, Quinn places her hand on my forearm and gives me a little smile as the sound of the call connecting fills my ears.

Not more than thirty minutes later Eddie follows Lauren and Ben into the flat. Thankfully, Trey and Erica ran downstairs to get everyone something to drink seeing as our kitchen is basically empty. Before long we've all placed our food orders and are sitting back on the sofas with drinks in hand. Erica sulks as she looks at the glasses of wine in both Quinn and Lauren's hands seeing as she's unable to drink and has to put up with a glass of cloudy lemonade. Eddie looks surprisingly at home with a beer as he talks to Trey about the education system. It's not something I thought Trey would be all that interested in, but I guess he needs to be seeing as he has two teenage daughters who'll be going through it all soon.

"So, are you going to be leaving us for better things once you've got a few certificates behind you?" Ben asks. He doesn't look as happy about the idea as I'm sure he would have done not so long ago. He hated me when he first came back, and rightly so. Lauren made it look like I'd stepped into his place when the side of the bed he abandoned was barely cold, but we've managed to build some kind of friendship now that Lauren's in his arms once again.

Thinking about reality is a sobering thought, one I'm not ready for. "I've no idea what I'm doing, man. It seemed like a good idea, and I guess it was because I met this one." I wrap my arm around Quinn's shoulders and pull her into me, kissing the top of her head. "But I've no idea what comes next."

"Well, we'll support you whatever you decide. If you want to go part-time so you can study or anything, all you need to do is ask. There are definitely opportunities for progression as long as the work keeps coming like it is if you'd like to stay in the industry."

"That means a lot. Thank you. But we'll see. I've got more important things to worry about now."

"I get that, man. I really do."

The evening is just like so many we've had in the past, aside from the obvious additions of Quinn and Eddie. I feel more like myself than I have in a long time. I hadn't realised the strain keeping my evening school and Quinn a secret were, but now it's all out there I feel like I can breathe again.

Once we've eaten, the girls insist on cleaning up, leaving me alone with the guys. While Eddie sits sipping on his beer, probably wondering what his life has become—at least he didn't turn up wearing his tie pin and pocket square—the three of us watch our girls as they clean, chat, and laugh. Quinn seems to have fitted in perfectly, and I couldn't be happier. Stories of her past are depressing at best; having a couple of girlfriends is exactly what she needs. I'm busy scheming up things I could plan for the three of them to do when Ben drags me from my thoughts.

"I never thought I'd see the day, you know?"

"Sorry, what?" Turning to look at him, I find amusement written all over his face.

"The day you looked at a girl like that." He nods over to where Quinn is and I can't help but follow his gaze. I just can't get enough of her. Her dark hair's been pulled back from her face with a couple of clips, and she's still wearing one of my hoodies over a pair of leggings. It's so fucking sexy. I look away as she goes to bend over to load the dishwasher because I don't need my boner trying to break through my joggers while I sit with these dickheads.

"You're just still shocked that I didn't fall for a guy. Don't even try to tell me you lot didn't have bets going on."

Ben holds his hands up in defence as Eddie blanches beside him. He clearly wasn't expecting me to openly announce that I've swung both ways in the past. My sexuality isn't something I'll ever hide, and I smile thinking that it'll just give him something else to judge me for, but all he does is shrug his shoulders and take another sip of his beer. Maybe I've proved that no matter who was in my past, Quinn's it for me now.

Quinn laughs at something, and my head snaps around to find her once more. A smile twitches my lips and my chest swells with everything I feel for her.

"Fucking hell, he's gonna beat us to it, isn't he?"

Turning back, I find Ben elbowing Trey in the ribs. Trey laughs, clearly having a better idea about what Ben's talking about than I do.

"You bought the ring yet?" I damn near spit out the beer I'd just tipped into my mouth.

"Ring? No."

"You've thought about it though, right?"

"I...uh..."

"You're so fucking whipped, man."

Ben and Trey joke about me falling for the teacher while Eddie sits nervously playing with his can. I'd figured out the first time I saw him with Quinn that he wanted her. I've no idea how he's feeling now aside from knowing that anything between the two of them is never going to happen. Or maybe he's just worrying about having a member of staff shagging a student. Who the fuck knows? He's so stiff and unreadable it's hard to get much from him.

"So what about you then?" Ben asks turning to Eddie. "Got a girl on the scene?"

"No, not currently." Ben's eyebrows rise at his posh tone.

"You're into girls though, right?"

Laughing to myself, I watch as Eddie's eyes almost pop out of his head at the suggestion.

"Yes. I'm very much into girls."

"You should come out with us sometime. I'm sure we'd find you a few willing candidates, right Joe?"

The image of some of the women I've met on nights out come to mind. They'd eat Eddie alive.

"No, no, I think I'm good," he says, sounding horrified by the suggestion.

"We'll see. You can't be the only single one in this little group."

The way Ben's accepted him kind of surprises me. Eddie's not really our kind of guy, but I guess he's thinking the same as me. If he's important to Quinn, he's just been baptised into this crazy little family we've got going on.

BY THE TIME we say goodbye to everyone and Ben's adamantly told us both that we've got to be at the work Christmas do he's organised next weekend, I'm so ready for a bit of one on one time with my girl.

"Your friends are—"

"Crazy, weird, completely fucking nuts?"

"I was going to say awesome, but yeah, I guess those work too." While we were locked in our little lodge, I'd given Quinn the rundown of each of my friends and how they got to where they are now so she'd have a little inside information ready for when she met them. From how well she got on with the girls, it seems my plan worked.

"Lauren and Erica invited me out for a shopping trip at the weekend, if you're okay of course," she adds quickly.

"Quinn, I am more than okay and perfectly able to look after myself for a few hours. You should go, get your new life started with a bang."

"I thought we'd already done that when we pulled my first all-nighter."

"Oh yeah, that night went with a bang all right."

The image of her falling apart beneath my hands once again fills my mind and my cock swells. Lifting my hands so my palms cup her breasts, I squeeze until she lets out a little moan of pleasure.

"But your—"

"I'm fine, Quinn. Stop worrying and let us take what we both need. Plus," I add, a salacious smile forming on my lips, "you can do all the work."

"Oh, can I?"

"Fuck yeah. I wanna watch you ride me." My heart pounds and my blood reaches boiling point as it all heads south. "Come on. Let's christen our new home." Taking her hands in mine, I pull her down to the bedroom.

The second we're in the room, I reach for the hem of my hoodie and pull it up and over her head, revealing her thin t-shirt. That soon follows and lands in a pile on the floor so I can suck her nipples into my mouth. Her taste explodes on my tongue, and I'm reminded once again that I'm probably never going to get enough.

Kissing down her stomach, I push her leggings from her legs before standing and making quick work of my clothes. The second I'm naked, I fall down onto the bed and stretch out, waiting for her to do her worst.

"You sure about this?" She chews on her fingernail as her eyes run the length of me. They linger on my cock, telling me that although she's questioning this, she wants it just as badly as I do.

"Get the fuck up here."

She crawls onto the bed, going to settle herself over my waist, but that wasn't what I had in mind—not yet, anyway.

Wrapping my hands around her waist, I lift her until she's straddling my face.

"Oh."

"Oh fucking right." I pull her hips down so she's at the perfect distance to be able to tease with the tip of my tongue, but I don't allow her to fall. It's been forever since I was inside her, and the next time she comes she's going to be full to the brim with my cock.

"Joe, please," she begs when I pull my fingers from her just before she reaches the point of no return.

Unable to wait any longer, I allow her to crawl down my body before resting my arms out and allowing her to take control. She wastes no time in wrapping her hand around my cock and guiding me to her entrance.

We both gasp as we connect for the first time in weeks. My entire body locks up with pleasure as she slowly sinks down onto me, her pussy clenching tighter with every inch she takes.

"Fucking perfect," I moan as I watch her start to move. She's slow and gentle. I know she's worried about hurting me and splitting my stitches, but I'm determined to drive her so crazy that she forgets.

Unable to only watch, I grab on to her hips and force her lower so I can grind into her. She cries out my name, and, exactly as I intended, she ups her tempo. Her tits bounce as she drops down harshly on me, desperate to find the release I kept her on the edge of all this time.

Just before she falls, her hands lift and she

takes her breasts, squeezing her nipples between her fingers.

"Fuck, Quinn. So fucking hot. So fuck—" I don't get to say any more because her pussy squeezes me so fucking tight that it sends me over the edge with her.

She rides out every last second of our pleasure before falling down onto me. Our chests heave, our hot skin sticking together, but I couldn't imagine anything better. Her weight gets heavier as she relaxes and I have to shift slightly when my stomach starts to ache.

"Shit, am I hurting you?"

"I'm perfect. You're fucking perfect."

She shifts her weight off me but we don't lose our contact as we both drift off to sleep.

I want to say that being back in London means Quinn gets a full night's rest, but it's far from that. If anything, her night terrors are worse. She's refused to talk about her nightmares, but I don't need to hear her words to know what they're about. If things don't start improving then I fear I'm going to have to push her to talk—whether that's to me or a professional. Only time will tell.

CHAPTER TEN

The smile that lights up Quinn's face when she fights her way into the flat, laden down with bags after her shopping trip with the girls, is everything.

She walked out of the house this morning leaving me with a raging hard on after she got herself all dressed up for her day out. Her excitement was infectious and her joy now is exactly the same. Anyone else would think she has nothing to worry about, but I see her concern when she thinks I'm not looking. I recognise the extra makeup she's using to cover the dark circles under her eyes.

"I'm assuming you've had a good day."

"It's been incredible. My feet hurt!"

"Sit down and I'll get you a coffee."

"Wine?" she asks with a laugh.

"Sure thing. Wine coming right up."

Hearing that my suspicions were correct about her never having had a girly day out before confirmed what I was thinking about ensuring she gets to do it all now. She might have given me her London bucket list the night I took her out, but I think in reality there's a lot more that needs to go on it.

Taking her glass over, I fall down onto the sofa next to her and allow her to show me everything she bought.

By the time she's been through all the bags, there's a towering pile of clothes, shoes, and handbags, not to mention lingerie that I'm dying to see her in, on the coffee table in front of us.

"Whoa, how much did you spend?"

"I've no idea. Do you have any idea how good it is to say that?"

Having lived quite a bit of my life with absolutely nothing to my name, I agree, knowing exactly how she must be feeling.

The solicitor Eddie set her up with to deal with her divorce proceedings came over yesterday seeing as they'd only been speaking on the phone the last couple of weeks and explained the process, and if everything goes as he's planning then she shouldn't need to worry about money for a very long time. Which brings us to the elephant in the room.

Her job.

As if she can read my mind, she rests back on the sofa, takes a sip of her wine and turns to me.

"I don't think I want to go back to work." She says the words in a rush like she's not sure what my response is going to be. "I mean, I want to work, but I don't think I want to go back to my old job."

"Okay."

"Okay?"

"Of course. We've got a place to live, I've got a job that pays pretty well, and you've got some money. Why would it be an issue?"

"I just—" Her face pales.

Taking her free hand in mine, I stare into her eyes to ensure she hears every word I say. "I'm not him, Quinn. My priority is you and your happiness. I don't care if I have to work double to allow you to do whatever it is you want. I'll do anything it takes to make you happy."

Tears fill her eyes and I catch the first one that falls with my thumb. She nods but doesn't say anything for a minute or two.

"What about you? You're going back to school, right?"

"I'd like to, but like I said, it's not my priority right now. Anyway, Eddie might not even have me back."

"I'm sure he will. Let's invite him round for dinner and we'll sweet talk him into letting you back. Probably best to do that before I resign. I'll help you catch up on what you've missed while I look for a new job."

"What do you want to do?"

"I still want to work with kids, but I'm not totally sure."

"We'll figure it out."

She relaxes into my side and breathes me in. I want to bite my tongue and follow her lead, ignoring the elephant in the room, but knowing it's in her best interest, I sit up and look down at her.

"W-what's wrong?" Her brows draw together, sensing that I'm about to say something that she's not going to like.

"I think...I think you should see someone about what happened."

"I'm fine, Joe. This isn't the first time I've had nightmares. They'll get better."

"But what if they don't? I'm worried about you."

She blows out a long breath as I stare at her, pleading with her to do the sensible thing. She keeps playing off what happened like it was an everyday thing, but it wasn't. It's something she needs to deal with before it takes over our lives and he continues to have control over her.

"Okay," she whispers. "Okay. I'll look into it."

"Thank you," I say, a huge wave of relief washing through me. I want us to start our lives together properly, not with him hanging over us. We've still no idea if he's going to grant her the divorce she deserves; he shouldn't take her sleep too.

WE HAVE the most surreal week. Well, it's surreal to me because I've never done the domesticated thing before. Together we clean the flat and move the furniture around a bit to make it less Trey's place and more ours, and we go shopping for some little trinkets and cushions that Quinn says will make the place more homely. After being cooped up for the past week, it's incredible to get out of the house and get some exercise and fresh air. We fill the cupboards full of food and spend our nights cooking together. Quinn escorts me to the doctors to have my stitches out and to hear that I really am okay and should be able to go back to work soon, although only on light duties at first. I also hold her hand while she registers and books an appointment to get the ball rolling for her to get the help she needs. Her entire body trembled with fear, telling me that she was doing the right thing. She needs to deal with this properly, and as much as I wish I could be the one to fix everything, I know I'm not capable of it.

By the time the weekend rolls around we've fallen into our new life in our new home easily.

I leave Quinn to sleep in on Saturday morning seeing as she had a particularly bad night, and make our morning coffee. I tidy up a little from the night before, and when I walk back into the bedroom with steaming mugs in my hand her eyes flutter open.

"Good morning," I sing, my excitement getting the better of me.

"What's that smile for? Should I be scared?"

"Not at all. I've just got a surprise for you today."

"Oh?"

"I'm not telling you yet. It's a surprise."

"Fair enough." She pushes herself up the bed, the duvet falling to her waist and revealing her perfect, naked tits to me.

"On second thought, I might keep you in bed all day." Even though I was given the full go ahead from the doctor, Quinn is still keeping me on light duties in the bedroom it seems, despite the sexy lingerie that I know is hiding in her drawers. I'm fucking dying to take her exactly as I need her.

I hand her coffee over before climbing in beside her. She's silent for a few minutes as she chews on her bottom lip, deep in thought.

"What is it?" A small ball of dread fills my stomach. I hate it when she's obviously concerned about something, and this is most definitely one of those times.

Turning to me, I can see the tension in her features. Reaching out, I grab her free hand and squeeze in what I hope is support.

"Am I enough for you?" she asks quietly, casting her eyes away.

"What?" Grasping her cheek, I pull her back so she has no choice but to look into my eyes. Her blue ones start to swim with water as she waits for my response.

"Quinn," I breathe. "You're everything to me."

"But you used to—"

Guessing where she's going with this, I cut her off. "I was lost, Quinn. I went after whatever I could to try to find a place I belonged. It's the only way I knew. But it wasn't until you that I found where I was meant to be."

Her lip trembles as she reaches for me. "But the girls said—"

I laugh. "I should have known they were behind this."

"It's not their fault, they were just filling me in on some of your past...conquests."

"I'm not proud of my past, but I won't apologise for it. It was what it was. It distracted me when I needed it, but it's a part of who I am."

"I don't want you to apologise, Joe. I just want to know that you're not going to miss it. The men, the multiple partners."

Taking her mug from her hand, I place it on the bedside table and pull her down the bed, pushing the covers off in the process.

"Why would I miss that when I've got you?"

By the time we're both set for the day, she's

running late for her surprise, but at least we're both satisfied—for now at least.

"Who's that?" Quinn asks when the buzzer sounds out.

"Your surprise."

She quirks an eyebrow but goes for the door when I make no move to do so. She's greeted by Lauren and Erica asking if she's ready to go.

"Where are we going exactly?"

Walking over, I pass her a bag I'd already packed. "You're going to spend the day at the spa so you're ready for our big night out."

"Really?" she asks, sounding like a little girl who's just been told it's Christmas morning.

"Really. Here's everything you're going to need."

She squeals with excitement but ignores the bag I'm holding out in favour of jumping into my arms.

"I love you," she says softly into my neck as I hold her.

"I love you, too."

When I glance up, I find both Lauren and Erica staring at us with soppy smiles on their faces.

Releasing Quinn, I hand her the bag. "You

need to get going before these two start crying or some shit."

"It's the pregnancy hormones," Erica protests.

"Yeah, and what's her excuse?"

Lauren's mouth opens, but she doesn't get a chance to say anything.

"Oh my god, are you?"

"What? No! I'm just happy for Joe. I never thought he'd ever find someone to put up with his shit."

"Nice. Well, please try not to turn her off me before the end of the day, yeah?" I'm not really worried—there's nothing in my past that I'll hide from Quinn. There are probably a few things I'd rather explain myself instead of those two, but I trust them to know what to not say just quite yet, although if this morning's conversation is anything to go by it seems they haven't held back with divulging the number of sexual partners I've had.

No sooner have I closed the door behind Quinn after wishing her a good day than I'm opening it again to reveal the guys. The spa isn't the only surprise, although by the looks on their faces right now they're not as excited about this part as I am.

"What? Would you rather have gone to the

spa?" I ask as Ben and Trey stomp into the flat carrying everything we're going to need.

"No, a day at the pub would have been sufficient, but oh no, you've got us here fucking decorating," Ben moans, following Trey straight down towards the bedroom. "You owe us for this."

"Whatever," I mutter, going for the kitchen so I can feed the grumpy fuckers.

With their bacon under the grill, I go in search of my decorating party. The furniture is already in the centre of the room and they're putting dustsheets down.

"And you didn't want to just paint, you had to go for the fucking wallpaper, didn't you? Fucking hate wallpaper."

"What's got your knickers in a twist? Lauren refusing to put out?"

"Yes. She decided for some fucked up reason that we'd wait for Christmas. She read some shit in a magazine about delayed gratification. Fuck knows. All I do know is that Christmas better fucking hurry up and it had better be fucking good," he sulks much to our amusement. That is until I remember something.

"Aren't we all going away for Christmas?"

"Yep." A wide smile forms across his face.

"You'd better have a room at the other end of the house," Trey complains.

"Oh, like you can talk. I have it on good authority that this room's not all that soundproof. Isn't that right, Joe?"

"Correct. Although I doubt you two have heard a peep from us yet."

"You not getting any either?" My fingers twitch to wipe the smug as shit look off Trey's face.

"She's worried about my stitches."

"I thought you had them out?"

"I did," I groan.

"Maybe tonight's the night. Just wait until you knock them up, Erica can't get enough."

"Oh fuck off, you smug shit." Ben throws a paintbrush at Trey. He doesn't see it coming, and it connects with the side of his head.

"Chance would be a fine thing."

Before I know it, the smell of burning bacon filters down to us and two angry sets of eyes turn on me.

"You promised us breakfast. You'd better have more," Ben calls as I run from the room before the smoke alarm starts blaring.

Sadly, I don't have any more, but a quick visit to Uber Eats and I've got a breakfast made for kings on its way to the flat. They've agreed to help me pull a changing rooms job on our bedroom; the least I can do is feed them.

With the three of us barely stopping for breath, we manage to have the room papered, painted and put back into place with an hour to spare to meet the girls.

Ben races off home to get ready while Trey heads downstairs to do the same.

I stand in the doorway to our new bedroom and hope that I did the right thing. I know this place isn't where we've chosen to live, but with Quinn not returning to her job and not really knowing what she's going to do next, it might be where we live for a while yet so I want it to be as homely as possible for both of us.

Hoping I've achieved just that, I head for the shower and attempt to remove any evidence of paint from my body so she doesn't suspect anything.

Lauren's booked us a table at a fancy pants bistro for our work Christmas meal. The place looks like an old warehouse with all its pipework and ventilation being used as part of the decoration. All the fittings are copper and the lighting is a little dark as Trey and I make our way to the maître d'. He shows us to a private function room up a flight of stairs where I find a few of my colleagues who all come over to greet me and see how I am after I disappeared from work two weeks ago.

There are a few wives and girlfriends here already, but the one I'm desperate to see hasn't arrived yet.

"Should have known they'd be late," Ben says, coming over to join us with a handful of pints.

The minutes tick by before a silence falls over the room. Wondering what's going on, I look towards the door where everyone else seems to be staring and my breath catches in my throat.

Standing between Lauren and Erica is my girl, but she doesn't look anything like I've seen before.

Her hair has been styled into an edgy inverted bob, her eyes are dark and smoky, and her lips are fire engine red. But as breath taking as that is, it's the dress that I'm pretty sure has stopped every conversation in the small room. It's leather, low cut and skin fucking tight. It just about hides her breasts, nips her in at the waist and skims down her round hips and shapely thighs until it stops just below her knees, revealing milky calves and one serious pair of strappy fuck-me heels.

"Pretty sure your gentle lovin' is gonna end tonight, man," Ben whispers in my ear, but I barely register the words. I'm too lost to Quinn.

She doesn't look anywhere in the room but at me. A slightly unsure smile graces her lips and I just about manage to keep my feet rooted to the spot and not drag her off home before tonight's really begun. How the fuck am I meant to look at her like that and not do anything inappropriate?

Trey breaks the moment between us by dragging everyone's attention to him and Erica when he pulls her into his arms and slams his lips down on hers. We're in a room surrounded by people who know they're a couple—the public claiming of his girl is a little much, but each to their own.

Lauren disappears into Ben's side, together greeting people they saw only yesterday at work like it was a year ago. All the while I can't take my eyes off Quinn. My mouth waters, my muscles clenching with my need to go over and drag her out of here to be alone.

Eventually she gets impatient and she makes her way over.

"Hey."

"Hey, yourself." My eyes drop from hers,

taking in every inch of her and committing it to memory. "Did you have a good day?"

"It was incredible. Thank you so much."

"It was totally worth it. This dress is...fuck, I don't even know what it is. Where've you been hiding it? I'd have remembered if it was in your collection last weekend."

"Erica kept hold of it for me to surprise you."

"Well, I'm certainly surprised. Although I'm not all that impressed that every guy I work with is also seriously surprised by it."

"Better show them who I belong to then."

Challenge shines in her eyes. I wait for a beat until she thinks I'm not going to take her up on it before reaching for her waist. She lets out a squeal as we collide. I wrap my hand around the back of her neck and pull her lips to mine.

Shouts, catcalls and wolf whistles sound out behind me, but I pay my idiot co-workers no attention as I put all my focus into kissing my girl.

When I eventually pull back, her eyes are glistening with lust and her tits are swollen and fighting to get out of her dress. If it wasn't so fucking incredible to look at, I might want to make her change back into a twinset to ensure those babies are for my eyes only.

"Come on, we need to order," Lauren calls out behind me. After another two seconds we make our way to our seats.

I get a few winks and slaps on the back from the guys before they greet Quinn politely. I've known a few of these guys for a long time now. They know exactly what I'm like, seeing as we've been on more than a few nights out and heard me bang on and on about never getting tied down, but they all accept Quinn like she's a permanent part of my life—which I'm grateful for, because that's exactly what she is.

The meal's incredible and the service fantastic, but nothing is more mind-blowing than the woman sitting beside me. She joins in with everyone's conversations like she's known them all her life, she's charming and funny, and she has everyone wrapped around her little finger in mere minutes. It makes me so sad to think that the previous man in her life kept her locked up like she was in a fucking prison and stopped her enjoying herself like this.

"Are you okay? You've got a serious look in your eyes that I'm not sure I like," she asks when there's a break in the conversation.

"I'm good. Just trying to figure out what I did to deserve to have you sitting beside me."

She shrugs. "You decided to better your life and instead you found me."

"There's nothing instead about it. You have made my life better. Fuck it, you've *made* my life."

Her eyes soften as she smiles at me. I'm so close to telling her that we'll sack off the rest of the night in favour of heading home when Ben announces that we're on the move.

Everyone gets up and grabs their coats. A few of the older members of staff bid us farewell as they head off home for a mug of cocoa and their slippers, but the rest of us move to our usual haunt, The Avenue.

The last time I was here it was the night I've since discovered Quinn was watching me. She's told me more than once that she was jealous of the people I was dancing with that night and how we could just forget the world and enjoy ourselves. Well, I fully intend on giving her all of that. It might not be the one night-stand she wanted, but I have every intention of taking her home with me tonight.

After two rounds of shots bought by the boss, we head out to the dance floor. I waste no time in pulling her into me and moving with the beat of the music. She looks back at me and her smile is wider than I think I've ever seen it before. The realisation of how much weight has been lifted off her since the last time we were in a club hits me and I drop my lips to hers.

Turning in my arms, she tucks her hands into the back pockets of my trousers and pulls me tightly to her. I lose myself to her kiss and to the beat of the music.

I've done this a million times before, danced until I forgot the world around me, but having her in my arms feels like the first time I've ever done it. I meant what I said to her earlier: meeting her really did make my life. All the bullshit from my past melts away, my parents, my endless encounters with strangers as I tried to connect with someone in a way I didn't know I needed to. They all fade to nothing, and the only thing I can think about is my future with my girl.

We drink, we dance, and we laugh. Time seems to stand still as I enjoy my evening with my favourite people. At some point Eddie joined us. He was apparently meant to be spending the evening with his douchebag friends (Quinn's words, not mine) in the VIP section but instead decided to slum it with us peasants. At one point he even found himself a girl to dance with. Maybe there is more to him than meets the eye.

I've no idea what the time is, but in the end my need for Quinn gets the better of me. I've no idea what she's got hiding under that dress—if anything, it's so damn tight—but I can't wait any longer to find out.

"We're leaving. I've got somewhere better to be."

"Oh yeah?" she breathes in my ear.

"Yeah. Inside you."

Taking her hand, I lead her away from the dance floor and our friends.

"Shouldn't we tell them we're leaving?" She looks back over her shoulder in concern but everyone's too busy dancing to pay us any attention.

"They'll understand."

She nods slightly and allows me to pull her the rest of the way from the club. As we descend the stairs, I order us an Uber, and as if someone is looking down on us tonight, there's one right outside.

We climb in the second we spot it. If he says anything I don't hear it because the moment I close the door behind me, I pull Quinn into my side and continue what we started in the club.

My tongue slides past her lips and she moans quietly into my mouth, her need for me getting the better of her just like mine is for her.

The journey is over in a flash, although I'm not sure that's really true because the second my lips connect with Quinn's all sense of time seems to vanish.

We're out of the taxi and fumbling our way towards the lift before I've realised we've moved.

I slam my hand down on the button for the fourth floor and together we crash back against the wall. My hands run up her waist and squeeze her breasts, my need to have her naked almost has me ripping fabric from her body. Her fingers frantically pull at where my shirt's tucked into my trousers. The hot skin of her hands meets my abs, and I flinch at the sparks that shoot around my body.

Fuck, I hope I don't ever get used to that feeling.

I'm just aware enough to know when the lift door opens. I swing her up into my arms and carry her to the door. I've got it open and we're on our way towards the bedroom before I have time to blink. In my lust haze I've totally forgotten about her final surprise for the day, until she looks up at me and says, "What's that smell?"

"Just wait."

I drop her to her feet outside our closed bedroom door.

"Go on," I encourage.

She lifts her hand and pushes the handle down. The second the door swings open she gasps.

I left the bedside lights on along with the little fairy lights that are now hanging around the gold-framed mirror above the bed.

"Joe, it's beautiful."

Coming to stand behind her, I nuzzle her neck, drinking in her sweet scent.

"You said your office was cream and gold and that you loved it so..."

"It's perfect."

"I just wanted somewhere that felt like yours. That felt like home."

"This is my home, Joe. It's where you are."

"Fuck." I scoop her up and launch her at the bed. She squeals and giggles as she bounces, but she soon stops when I loom over her.

"You ready to properly christen your new home?" I flip her over before she can even answer and pull the zip of her dress down her back. She arches when my tongue follows its progress and I find exactly what I was expecting: no bra.

Pushing the fabric from her shoulders, I cup both her breasts, making her moan in pleasure.

"I hope you've got plenty of energy because you're not sleeping tonight until I've made you come every way. Starting with these." I pinch her nipples hard and her arse grinds against my erect cock.

I trail kisses down her back until I can't wait to have her taste on my tongue.

Flipping her on to her back, I pull her dress from her legs, leaving her sexy as fuck shoes in place. I have every intention of feeling those bad boys digging in my arse cheeks in the very near future.

Emotion chokes me as I stare down at her before me in just a tiny lace thong and her shoes.

How the fuck did I end up here with this incredible woman waiting for my touch?

"Fuck, I love you."

Ripping my shirt from my body, I toe off my shoes and drop my trousers. I leave my boxers on for now. If my cock touches her then my restraint is going to snap. I need her fucking begging for it before I slide on home.

Crawling up the bed, I kiss up her legs and her stomach before kissing around her breasts, teasing her until she's thrusting them into my face for more.

"Fucking love it when you're like this," I mutter before giving her what she needs and sucking one nipple after the other deep into my mouth.

She moans, her nails clawing at my back, and my control snaps. Finding her wet and needy centre, I thrust two fingers inside her, delighting when she clamps down and arches her back. I find her sweet spot while torturing her nipples with my tongue and teeth and in minutes she cries out my name. Lifting my eyes to her face, I watch as she falls apart. Her lips part, her cheeks flush, and her eyes close as she rides out the waves of pleasure, and my chest constricts with everything the sight does to me. I swear I could do this every fucking day for the rest of my life and it would never be enough. This woman beneath me is everything I had no idea I wanted, but I'm going to fucking well keep her.

CHAPTER ELEVEN

"What's wrong?" I ask the next morning when I emerge from the shower and find Quinn staring down at her phone, her forehead creased and bottom lip trembling, even though she's trying to contain it.

She lets out a sigh but doesn't look up. "He's refusing to sign."

"Fuck." I fall down beside her and pull her into my side.

"My lawyer has booked me an appointment to see him if I want to." I tense. The last thing I want is for her to have to look that monster in the face again.

"Do...do you want to?"

"No," she says, a sad laugh falling from her. "I

never want to see him again, but I need to move on. I need to close that chapter of my life and I can't do that while I'm still technically Mrs. Davenport."

I nod, unable to disagree. "Okay, so when are we going?"

"I've got to ring him back."

She stands, her fingers gripping her phone in a death grip. Silently she leaves the room, and my heart breaks for her. Things had just started improving. She's had two sessions with a therapist and a couple of peaceful nights, but I can't help thinking that seeing him will send her back to when it first happened.

She's only gone a few minutes at the most.

"We can go today."

"Today?" I ask, my eyes wide with shock.

"He'll pulled some strings for me. I want this sorted ASAP."

"Wow, okay. Are you sure you want to do this?"

She shrugs. "You don't have to come, I can do this alone."

"Fuck that, Quinn." I push myself from the edge of the bed and stand in front of her. I take her cheeks in my hands and bend slightly so I can stare into her eyes. "You never have to do anything alone again. You need to face him? Then we do it together. This is how things are now, Quinn. Us. Me and you."

She nods, tears forming in her eyes, but she doesn't allow them to drop.

Taking a step back, she turns toward the wardrobe. Wrapping my fingers around her wrist, I pull her back to me. "You change your mind at any point. You tell me and we'll turn around."

"I need to do this. I need those papers signed, but also, I think seeing him locked in there might help give me the closure I need."

"Okay, let's do this."

In only thirty minutes we're on the road. The drive to the prison is long and sadly mostly in silence as Quinn most probably relives her life with the man we're about to see. I hate that she's dealing with this on her own, but I'm confident that she'll say something if she needs me.

The prison itself is a massive red brick building with huge gates topped with barbed wire. After getting through security we find a place to park and sit and stare. Dread sits heavy in my stomach, I can only imagine how Quinn's feeling right now.

Reaching over, I take her hand. It trembles as I hold it tight in support.

"We can go back," I offer.

She shakes her head. "No. I can do this."

She blows out a long, slow breath before unbuckling and pushing the door open. The bitter wind immediately rushes into the car and makes me shiver. This place fills me with nothing but dread, and the dark and cold weather only makes it that much more unnerving.

Getting through to where others are waiting to meet their loved ones is harder work than getting through Heathrow, but after what feels like a year, we find ourselves a seat at a table and wait.

Glancing over at Quinn, I find her as white as a sheet as she worries the sleeve of her jumper, her eyes locked on the door a couple of the inmates have come through as she waits to see him again.

I know the second he appears because everything about her changes. The strong and confident woman I know and love almost vanishes before my eyes. I follow her stare, but if it weren't for her reaction then I never would have recognised him.

He's sporting a shiner of a black eye and a split lip. It's been weeks since I laid into him—that should have healed long ago. This is recent, and something settles inside me that he's not being treated the way I'm sure he expects to be in here.

"Elizabeth," he drawls, making my fingers curl into fists at my sides. "To what do I owe this pleasure?"

Quinn opens her mouth but no words pass her lips. My demand for him to set her free is right on the end of my tongue, but I bite it back. It's not my place to do this for her.

"I see you brought your security again. He should be rotting in here with me after his assault. What did you do? Pay off the cops or something? A thug like you shouldn't be walking the streets."

"That's enough," Quinn snaps, finding her voice at last. "Do not talk to him like that. He's more of a man than you'll ever be."

He laughs. It's bitter and evil. "Is that right?" His top lip curls in disgust as he looks me up and down. It's amusing because where I'm six foot two and built of solid muscle, he's a tall, skinny golf playing wanker. Even if he did stand up to me the day I found Quinn, he never would have won. Sadly, the only people he can beat are women and kids.

"I want a divorce, Jeremy. I need you to sign those papers and get it over with."

"Yeah, about that..." He taps his finger to his busted lip. "I don't want to."

Anger rolls off Quinn in waves.

"You're a fucking arsehole, you know that?" she seethes, careful to keep her voice down so she doesn't alert the guards.

His laugh has a shiver of terror racing down my spine. How Quinn lived with this cunt for so long and came out as stable as she has is a fucking miracle; the guy is nothing less than a total psychopath.

I lean forward, my teeth bared, the muscles in my neck straining with my restraint.

"Give her what she's fucking owed."

"Oh wow, the goon talks."

My teeth grind to the point I fear I might crack one.

"I do a fucking lot more than that. Top of my list is taking care of a woman as she deserves to be treated. Now sign the fucking papers and allow Quinn—Elizabeth—to get on with her life while you rot away in here."

"Never."

"What did I ever do to you for you to hate me so much?" Quinn asks, sounding genuinely curious.

He looks her up and down, making me want to wrap my hand around his neck. "I don't hate you, Elizabeth. I love you." His brows draw together as if this should be obvious to his wife, his eyes bounce between her like he's waiting for her to return the sentiment.

"Liar. You never loved me. The only thing you love is control. You never wanted me to stand up for myself. You always wanted me weak and put exactly in my place."

He shrugs. "Well, it seems like you've got me all figured out. Which leads me to wonder why you bothered making this trip. You're mine. You'll be mine for as long as I can keep you, so you can forget about your precious divorce. You'll have to kill me before I sign those papers."

"I'm sure that can be arranged," I mutter, barely keeping myself together.

"Fine. Have it that way. Divorce or not, you no longer control me. You no longer have that power. Goodbye, Jeremy. I hope you have a fucking horrible stay and get everything you deserve." With that, she pushes her chair out behind her and stalks towards the exit.

"Sign those fucking papers," I hiss. "I see the guys giving you the eye in here. They clearly haven't held back." I nod at his face. "And that's only from a couple of weeks here. I'm sure I could find a way to make your life a living hell. You're in here with the worst of the worst, I'm sure they'll take great delight in wiping an abuser and paedophile from the planet." I don't hang around for his response. I need to get to my girl.

The second I step from the room she runs at me, tears staining her cheeks. I open my arms and wrap her in them as she cries.

"I knew it was a stupid idea."

"You had to at least try. But like you said, it doesn't matter. He can't rule your life now. We'll just wait him out. Your life can move on with or without his consent."

She nods against me, but I'm not sure if she believes me. We've not really talked about where our relationship is headed, but I have every intention of asking her to be my wife one day. I'd like that to be one day soon, but I'll wait forever to hear her say 'I do' if I have to.

The drive home is almost as silent as the trip up, but Quinn seems different. She might not have got what she needed, but I think she was right. Seeing him in there, without his freedom...it was the closure she needed.

OUR NEW LIFE together continues as if the trip to the prison never happened. Quinn doesn't really mention it, but now she's got her answer she's relaxed somewhat. So what if we have to wait five years for her to be a free woman? It'll be worth it.

With only a week before we head off to the Cotswolds to celebrate Christmas as one big, dysfunctional family, Quinn insists on doing something that I've never been all that fussed about, decorating the flat before Eddie comes round for her to admit that she's not returning to work. Lauren used to somehow manage to get me to help her, usually with blackmail of some kind that involved a night out and free alcohol, but this year I'm actually looking forward to doing something so normal.

We spend almost an entire day shopping for everything we're going to need. Quinn oohs and ahhs for hours over what colour theme she wants before eventually deciding not to have one and just going all traditional.

My van looks like Santa's thrown up inside it by the time we head towards home ready to put it all in place. I've got a giant arse tree strapped to the top, which makes everyone we pass look our way.

Even with a working lift it takes us three trips to get everything up to the flat.

"Have you got a Christmas playlist on your phone?" Quinn asks, putting the bag full of mulled wine, mince pies and dinner ingredients in the kitchen.

"Do I look like the kind of guy who has a Christmas playlist?"

"Scrooge!" she calls back while I pull up something along the lines of what she's after and hit play.

The beginning of 'Step into Christmas' fills the flat and she immediately starts wiggling her hips in time with the music.

I think I'm going to enjoy the next few hours.

With the music blaring, we turn the flat into Santa's grotto and by the time we're waiting for Eddie to arrive, lights twinkle, the festive candle Quinn picked up along with her cooking fills the air, and it all takes me back to a time where I was so innocent I had no idea what my life was really like and when I actually enjoyed family Christmases. I was probably four or five, and the thought of it being twenty years since I enjoyed this time of the year sits heavy in my chest.

"What's wrong?" Quinn asks, making me jump as she wraps her arms around my waist and presses her face between my shoulder blades. I instantly relax.

"Just thinking about my childhood."

"Do you have any good memories?"

"A few. Before my parents showed their real colours. You?"

"Same, although I think I had a few more years than you did. But at the same time, I wasn't brave enough to get out when things started going south."

"None of that matters now." Spinning her around so I've now got my arms around her waist and my chin resting on the top of her head, we both stare at the twinkling lights of the tree. "My life started the day I walked into your classroom. The world is our oyster. We can make our own memories, our own families, our own happiness."

"That sounds perfect. This is going to be the best Christmas ever."

"Just the first of many, babe."

She looks back over her shoulder at me and just as I'm about to press my lips to hers, the buzzer goes off.

"Cock blocker," I mutter much to Quinn's amusement as she walks over to the door to let Eddie in.

We're instructed to sit at the table while Quinn finishes off dinner. Eddie chats away about something, probably something boring he read in The Times, but I'm too distracted watching Quinn move about in the kitchen and bending over to pull the chicken out of the oven.

"Are you even listening?" he snaps, dragging my attention back.

"Honestly, no, not a fucking word."

"I hope you're a better student than dinner guest."

"I don't know if my teacher will agree."

"Pain in the arse," is called from the kitchen.

"The woman doesn't lie."

Eddie falls quiet as Quinn brings our plates over and we start to tuck in.

"This is incredible, thank you."

"It's the least I can do after everything you've done for me."

Awkwardness settles as we all avoid the giant elephant sitting in the spare chair.

"So...what are you two planning on doing, because you can't exactly—"

"I'm not coming back," Quinn blurts and then breathes a huge sigh of relief.

"Oh."

"I'm sorry, but after everything, I think I just want to do something different. I love teaching, you know that, but I need a break or something."

"Understandable. And what about you? Am I expecting you to be back in class in the New Year?" Eddie turns his eyes on me.

"If you'll have me."

"I'll certainly consider it," he says, but a smile twitches at his lips as he tries to stay serious.

"You're teaching my evening class?"

"Yeah, I had to shift things around when you didn't come back. I was the only one who could do it. They're a pretty good class. I've picked up a couple of your day lessons too."

"You've been missing the worst student."

"Is this all I'm going to get if I come back?"

"Yeah, probably."

It's nice to see a different side to Eddie, the one Quinn probably got to know all those years ago instead of the judgemental arsehole I first encountered. I'm sure he's got his reasons to dislike how I look, just like I have for how he chooses to dress. Maybe we've even got something in common if I were to press the issue, but that's not something for this pre-Christmas get-together.

The conversation moves on to other things and it's not until we're sitting on the sofas later in the evening that Quinn brings up work again. They start discussing which classes he's taken over and they go through a few students while I refill our drinks.

"Tell me about Jodie Attington." Eddie leans forward, his elbows on his knees, looking more interested in this one than the others they've talked about.

"Oh um... I don't know a lot other than the report I filed. I'm assuming you've read that?"

"I have. She just looks so sad, so lost. I don't know, there's just something about her."

"Watch out, sounds like Mr. Richards is getting a little too interested in a student," I say with a laugh, expecting him to do the same, but instead all the colour drains from his face.

"I'm...I'm just concerned for her welfare."

Quinn gives me a look that screams 'shut the hell up', and I busy myself with my drink while she explains the bruises and suspicions she has. I immediately feel awful for making a joke of the situation when this girl is obviously having a shit time of it.

"I'll miss students like her. Knowing I was making a difference to students whose lives were spiralling out of control around them was one of the things that got me out of bed in the morning."

"I'm sure you'll find loads of opportunities to work with kids like that in this city. Even some voluntary mentoring or something."

Quinn's eyes light up at the suggestion. She nods. "I'm going to look into that. I love the idea of helping students who've not had the kind of upbringing I did—not that it all turned out so great in the end."

"You'll be incredible at it," I say, dropping down and placing a kiss to her temple.

Eddie watches the interaction between us with intrigue filling his face.

"I've got to say that I wouldn't have put you two together in a million years. But sitting here now, student/teacher issue aside, you're kind of perfect together."

"Aw, are you going all soft on us?" Quinn asks light-heartedly.

"Well, obviously I'll never approve. I bet he doesn't even own a tie pin."

"Fucking right I don't, just like I'm sure you don't have any tattoos."

He swallows, a sly smile forming on his lips. "Actually, I do." We both stare at him, mouths agape. "I am not showing either of you two though."

"I told you he was a square," I say, elbowing Quinn in the ribs lightly.

"On that note, I think it's time I left."

We say goodbye and wish each other a merry Christmas and a happy New Year before Quinn closes the door behind him.

"There's no way he's got a fucking tattoo."

Chuckling, she steps away from me but I wrap my fingers around her wrist and pull her back.

"The cleaning can wait. I think it's time you taught your student a lesson," I whisper in her ear. She wants to chastise me, I can sense it, but her body shudders with desire. "I'll even let you grade me."

"You're impossible."

"You love it." I throw her over my shoulder and march her towards our bedroom. I've no idea if Erica and Trey are in downstairs, but I have every intention of giving them a taste of their own medicine. Hours of it.

EPILOGUE

Three months later...

Christmas was everything I hoped it would be and more. The six of us ate, drank, laughed, and made memories together. The holidays are for family, and that's exactly how we spent it.

The day before we left the flat, I found Quinn writing a Christmas card. I was a little surprised seeing as she'd quite happily left her old life behind and I wasn't aware of anyone in her new life she'd want to send one to that we hadn't already.

When I peered over her shoulder, a smile curled at my lips. She was writing to her mum. I'd broached the subject a couple of times about her reaching out. There was something that didn't sit right with me after her visit to the hospital, and I couldn't help feeling that both of them were in a similar position and could support each other, build a connection and find some light in the dark situation they'd been in.

"I might not send it," she admitted when she realised she had company.

"I'm proud of you for even writing it, babe." She smiled and stuffed it into her bag before we left the flat. Not ten minutes into the journey out of London and she demanded I pull over. Thinking something was wrong, I turned to her but she was already half out of the van. I left her to it and watched as she ran to a post box sitting on the pavement. She sucked in a large breath before popping the envelope through the hole.

"I've no idea if she even still lives at the house, but I feel better now," she admitted as I pulled away from the curb.

She didn't mention it the whole time we were away, but I could tell it was playing on her mind.

The first thing she did the second we stepped foot back in our building was to check the post. Sure enough, amongst the flyers and crap there was a Christmas card. Clutching it to her chest, I followed her up to the flat so she could open it.

It turned out her mum had moved, but the new residents had forwarded it on to her. She was living with a widowed friend as she tried to figure out what to do with her life now her husband was behind bars and her daughter at the other end of the country.

I'm pleased to say that since then they've been working hard to rebuild their relationship, and Quinn's even convinced her mum to come and stay with us in a couple of weekends' time.

I went back to both work and evening school when the new year started, and Quinn set out on her quest to find her new job and continued her regular therapy sessions. As she predicted, her nightmares had improved but they still happened most nights, and I wasn't letting her get away without the help she needed.

She's had a few interviews but as of yet she's not received the call she's been waiting for. She's got time though and she's got money to keep her going, plus what I'm earning. Things are pretty much perfect; there's only one little thing left to make our lives complete right now, and I intend on putting that straight tonight. And Quinn has no idea.

Quinn

I'm sitting on the sofa looking through job sites, hoping my perfect job will jump out at me and waiting for Joe to come home from his evening class. I was not expecting the manila envelope that arrived this morning. Since our trip to the prison, I tried to put thoughts of Jeremy ever signing our divorce to the back of my mind. Joe was right. He was out of my life and no longer had a say in how I lived. Five years was nothing in the grand scheme of things. It taunts me from the coffee table. My stomach knots as I think about showing Joe. I'm no longer a wife, no longer Mrs Elizabeth Quinn Davenport. I am at last free to live the life I've always wanted. I'm free to consider where my relationship with Joe could go. I never want to forget this feeling buzzing in my veins.

I made sure Joe had caught up on what he'd missed by the time his first class of the year rolled around, and just like I expected he got straight back to it and has produced some great work, none of which I've helped with. I've no doubt that he's got a bright future ahead of him if he keeps his head down and continues working hard.

It doesn't matter how much money I've got

sitting in my bank account, I still feel guilty that he's the only one with a job. I've done some voluntary work, but even that didn't quite hit the right mark. I know that job is out there somewhere, I just need to find it.

Looking at the clock, I've still got over thirty minutes until he's back. I've got our dinner prepared but there's not much I can do until he's here. My phone buzzes and I reach to grab it off the arm of the chair.

Joe: There's a box in my wardrobe.

My brows draw together as I stare at his cryptic message. Pushing myself from the sofa, I go in search of it.

Pulling the door open on his side of the wardrobe, I find it immediately with a note on the top.

Wear me.

A little laugh falls from my lips when I remove the lid and find the outfit he bought me the night he took me out to fulfil some of my bucket list. Memories hit and heat blooms in my chest. Even that first night I knew there was something between us, although I never could have imagined what was to come and how close it would bring us.

Pulling out the skinny black jeans and the barely there silver top, I make quick work of changing and doing my hair and make-up. I'm just putting my lipstick on when another text arrives.

Joe: Fancy a coffee?

I can't keep the smile off my face. I know exactly where he's asking me to go. I also know that if Eddie catches him texting in class, he's going to rip him a new one. The most unlikely friendship might be forming between them, but no one stands in Eddie's way or breaks his rules when he's teaching, even his budding new best friend.

Finding my shoes, I book an Uber and race out of the building, now desperate to see him. It seems like a year ago that he kissed me goodbye before leaving for class.

As usual, the traffic is horrendous trying to get across the city, but eventually I make it to the coffee shop. I step inside, expecting to find him waiting for me, but the only people here are busy with their own lives.

My stomach drops with disappointment that he's not here yet and I stand in line to order our drinks.

I'm lost in my own thoughts as a shiver runs down my spine. "Cappuccino, one sugar, chocolate sprinkles," is whispered in my ear, and I step back to lean into him. His warmth engulfs me as his lips find the skin of my neck.

"What's all this about?" I ask once we're seated.

"Thought it was time we had another crazy night."

"I don't need all that now. I've got you to keep me on my toes."

"You might not need it, but you deserve a good night out."

I can't really argue with that so I smile at him and sip my coffee.

"Plus, if I remember rightly there was something on your to do list that you never ticked off."

I laugh. "I'm not having a one-night stand."

"Damn fucking right you're not."

I try racking my brain for what other word vomit fell from my mouth that night, but I don't get the chance to figure it out because Joe stands and hold a hand out for me. "Ready to paint the town red?"

"So ready."

We take the tube into the centre of London, and I'm not surprised when he drags me to the Chinese takeaway we came to last time and orders the exact same dishes. We sit in Leicester Square and polish off every single bit as we sit, people watching. The little trip down memory lane is exactly what I didn't know I needed.

"Joe, I need to tell you something," I admit, ready to explode with excitement.

"Okay, go on." I hate that there's a little hesitation in his voice.

"I got some surprise mail this afternoon." His eyebrows rise. "I'm free."

"You're what?" His brows draw together, but I can see a little bit of hope sparkling in his eyes.

"I'm free. He signed."

"He signed?" he echoes.

"He did. I'm free."

Joe's up before I have a chance to blink. He pulls me from my seat and spins me around right in front of all the people in the square. I can't help the joy bubbling up my throat and I laugh as he continues. When he eventually set me on my feet, I sway with dizziness.

His eyes search mine, but he doesn't say anything. A little disappointment finds its way in. I hadn't realised that I was hoping he'd drop to one knee instantly and demand I become his, but that's exactly how I feel. Swallowing it down and forcing myself to enjoy the moment, I stare back at him.

"So what's next? Comedy club, live music and getting me off in a nightclub?"

His eyes darken with lust at my last suggestion. "Sounds like a pretty damn perfect night to me."

With our hands connected, Joe leads us in the direction we went that night. We visit all the same places and drink all the same drinks. The whole evening is incredible, just like I knew it would be, and although I have fond memories of the first time, tonight is even better.

The differences are stark.

I'm no longer scared for my life, no longer looking over my shoulder or fighting the growing connection between us. Tonight, I let go. I laugh like I have no cares in the world, and I knock back slippery nipples and screaming orgasms like a pro. And when he pulls me to him on the dance floor towards the end of the night, I don't tense, I don't worry if we're going to be caught, because I know without a doubt that this man is mine and there's not a damn thing anyone can do about it. The only thing I care about right now is being in his arms and making sure he never lets go.

The music pounds around us as we move in time to the music. Our hips roll, our skin is covered in a sheen of sweat and the alcohol we've consumed is making my head spin, but I zone out everything bar him and this moment.

His hands rest on my ribs just inside my top, but unlike last time they don't venture any higher, although it must be killing him to do so. Things are different this time. The lust simmering just below the surface ready to explode within both of us is still there, but we've learned to contain it, if only just. I've no doubt that Joe's restraint is going to snap any moment and I'm going to be dragged home to finish off the night properly. Not that there will be any complaints from me.

It can't be five minutes after I have that thought that he leans into my ear and suggests we leave. Excitement bubbles in my belly for what's to come, and I eagerly take his hand when he offers it, following him from the club.

He helps me into my jacket and together we

walk out into the night. It's still dark although there are signs of the approaching morning. London's commuters start a hell of a lot earlier than I was ever used to living in the country. Taxis zip past us, and others pour from clubs and bars ready to head home, probably to get ready for work like Joe's going to have to do in about two hours.

"Where are we going?" I ask when he ignores the cars lining the pavement and heads farther into the city.

"Breakfast," he says like it's the most obvious thing in the world. I try to bite back my disappointment that he's not taking me home to have me for breakfast. We've got the rest of our lives for that, I guess.

He takes us to a 24/7 diner and we fill up on greasy food before he sets off again until he slows in front of a dark building with a pink neon sign out the front.

"What's this place?" I crane my neck to see the sign properly. *Rebel Ink. Tattoo studio.*

"Joe?" I ask, my voice cracking slightly, although I'm unsure if it's with fear or excitement.

"I'm pretty sure this was on your list, and I wouldn't want you missing out on something you've always wanted."

"I was talking crazy that night."

"No you weren't. You want to be a rebel, and this is the place to be. I also happen to know that inside that building awaits the best damn tattoo artist this city has ever seen just waiting for us."

"Really?"

"Well, I think so. You ready?"

"Um...no."

He laughs but presses the bell beside the door nonetheless.

"What fucking time do you call this?" the guys asks even before the door's open.

"Sorry, got a little carried away with ourselves."

"Fucking pain in the arse."

I laugh to myself but follow Joe's lead when he gestures for me to step inside.

My eyes widen slightly when I get a look at the guy who's just let us in. I'd have thought he'd be an older biker type guy with no bare skin on show, a massive beard and a biker jacket, but instead I'm greeted by a young blonde guy who clearly looks after himself. He's wearing a long-sleeved black t-shirt so I don't get a chance to see what ink he's got, if any.

"Quinn, this is Zach. Zach, this is my girl, Quinn."

"Nice to meet you." He nods at me and turns towards a small room the back. I guess we're meant to follow.

"Up you get then," he encourages once we're all in the room.

"Uh..."

My heart hammers in my chest, but excitement gets the better of me. It's helped by the look of awe in Joe's eyes.

"I know you've thought about this more than you've ever let on. So, up you get," he says with a laugh.

He's right of course, not that I tell him.

"What's it going to be then?"

Sucking in a deep breath, I prepare to explain what I've been dreaming about for years. I never wanted anything big or fancy, just something to remind me of the life I made for myself out of the disaster I found myself in the middle of.

"I'd like some flying birds on my wrist. Not big...like this..." Pulling my phone from my bag, I find the image I've had on there for months just in case I ever got brave enough to put myself in this position."

"Consider it done. Lie back."

"Can't say I'm not relieved that you didn't want that somewhere more intimate."

Zach laughs at Joe's alpha caveman appearance. "Nothing fazes me now, man. I've pretty much done and seen everything."

I shudder at the thought while he sets up.

"You still want what we talked about?" Zach asks Joe.

"I do," he states proudly.

Something stirs inside me at the thought of getting to sit and watch Joe get inked.

I'm soon distracted from the thought as a buzzing fills the room and the first scratch of the needle hits me.

"Fuck."

Zach looks at me from the corner of his eye. The words *don't be a pussy* are right on the tip of his tongue, I can practically hear them.

Joe takes my hand and I squeeze it as Zach sets to work.

It stings, but actually it's not all that bad. It certainly wasn't painful enough to put me off considering another.

Once I'm wrapped up, we switch places after Joe's lowered his braces and undone his shirt. My mouth waters at the amount of skin he reveals, my earlier lust hitting me full force.

He lies back like he's done it a million times, which of course he has.

Zach gets himself ready before hovering his gun over Joe's left pec.

I watch, completely fascinated as Zach draws on his skin. His hand in the way means I don't really get to see what he's creating until he's finished and Joe sits up.

They both stare at me as I get my first look at the stunning artwork.

"Holy shit," I screech when it dawns on me what he's just done. "That's my name."

Joe grins while Zach just slaps his shoulder. I'm not sure if he's telling him he's an idiot or not, because it's kind of what I want to do. He's just had my name permanently tattooed over his heart.

"You like it?"

"I'm in shock and feel slightly bad that I didn't even consider your name and just got birds."

He laughs. "There's always time, babe."

Once he's dressed again we say our thanks to Zach, who sets about closing up for the night—or morning—to head home.

Joe still doesn't order us a taxi and we once again walk. Eventually the Thames appears in front of us. I'm assuming that Joe's got a destination in mind but at no point do I ask. I just enjoy his company. The tattoo on my wrist burns but I welcome it, a reminder of everything that got me to this point in my life.

We walk along the west bank until Joe heads towards Millennium Bridge and starts to cross.

"Where are we going?"

"We're nearly there."

I keep walking, ignoring the aching of my feet and wishing I'd thought to bring some flats.

We're halfway across when he suddenly stops and turns to me.

"What are you doing?"

"Enjoying the view."

"You should probably be watching the sunrise over the buildings then," I say with a laugh, but at no point does he take his eyes from me.

He sucks in a deep breath and swallows.

Wait...is he nervous?

I open my mouth to demand he tells me what's going on when he suddenly drops down onto one knee.

My eyes open so wide I fear they might be

about to pop out of my head as he reaches into his pocket and pulls out a small black box.

Holy shit.

"Quinn, I never ever thought I'd be doing this. I spent most of my life trying to find a piece of me that I didn't know I was missing, and then when I met you everything fell into place. My past slipped away and the only thing I could see was my future. *Our* future. I don't want to spend another day without you by my side. You've taught me so much more than any English lesson I could ever attend. You've taught me what true love is, what it truly means to put someone else first and to hope like hell they feel the same.

"My life started the day I walked into your classroom, and I don't want to live another day without you.

"So...if you'll have me, will you do me the greatest honour of agreeing to be my wife?"

A sob rumbles up my throat and the tears filling my eyes fall down onto my cheeks. I watch him pull open the box in his hand and reveal the most stunning and unique engagement ring I think I've ever seen in my life.

"Is that a black diamond?" I ask, reaching for it, not believing what I'm seeing. The princess cut black gem is cushioned in a rose gold band. It's breath taking and so Joe. It's just more proof that he gets me. He understands the rebel inside me and allows me to set her free.

"Is that a yes?"

"Of course it's a yes. A million times yes."

He's up from the pavement and has me in his arms in a second. He spins us around, clinging to me so slightly I worry my ribs might be about to crack.

"I love you so fucking much, Quinn."

"I love you, too." His lips find mine and as the sun rises behind us we celebrate the next chapter of our lives. Together.

I never wanted a white knight, and it turns out that the bad boy in the dirty work van was exactly what I needed.

Are you ready for Zach's story?
Hate You is a angst-filled, emotional and steamy
enemies to lovers romance.

ONE-CLICK NOW or continue reading for a
sneak peek.

ACKNOWLEDGMENTS

Originally, Ben's story was meant to be just one standalone to finish off my Falling series, I never expected it to take the turn it did but I'm so glad that it did. I've loved discovering more about these beautifully broken characters, and Joe and Quinn were no exception. I knew Joe would have an interesting story to tell from the moment he appeared in Losing the Forbidden and I was so excited to discover it.

I can't believe at almost eight months after publishing the first book in the Forbidden series that I'm now writing this on the final one. It's sure been a rollercoaster of a few months.

I've got so many people I need to thank. My awesome betas, Deanna, Lindsay, Suzanne and Tracy. Samantha, my PA, who I've no idea how I lived without. Evelyn, my editor, who puts up with my ramblings and makes them make sense. Paige, for proofreading and making sure each book's been as polished as possible. James Critchley and his mouth-watering models, George, Danny, and Daniel for gracing the covers and being the perfect guys for my characters.

And finally, you for being on this journey with me and supporting me all the way. I couldn't do any of this without you, so THANK YOU!

So, what's next? Well, you might recognise Zach the tattoo artist as Harrison's younger brother in His Manhattan. I loved him from the moment I wrote him back in 2017, and he's been nagging me ever since for his own book. Well...that's next. A brand new series focused on his tattoo studio, Rebel Ink. It'll be releasing spring 2020 and I can't wait to share more with you about it. Make sure you're in my reader group and signed up to my newsletter to be first to find out all the sexy details.

Until next time,

Tracy xo

ABOUT THE AUTHOR

Tracy Lorraine is a *USA Today* and *Wall Street Journal* bestselling new adult and contemporary romance author. Tracy has recently turned thirty and lives in a cute Cotswold village in England with her husband, baby girl and lovable but slightly crazy dog. Having always been a bookaholic with her head stuck in her Kindle, Tracy decided to try her hand at a story idea she dreamt up and hasn't looked back since.

Be the first to find out about new releases and offers. Sign up to my newsletter here.

If you want to know what I'm up to and see teasers and snippets of what I'm working on, then you need to be in my Facebook group. Join Tracy's Angels here.

Keep up to date with Tracy's books at
www.tracylorraine.com

ALSO BY TRACY LORRAINE

Falling Series

Falling for Ryan: Part One #1

Falling for Ryan: Part Two #2

Falling for Jax #3

Falling for Daniel (A Falling Series Novella)

Falling for Ruben #4

Falling for Fin #5

Falling for Lucas #6

Falling for Caleb #7

Falling for Declan #8

Falling For Liam #9

Forbidden Series

Falling for the Forbidden #1

Losing the Forbidden #2

Fighting for the Forbidden #3

Craving Redemption #4

Demanding Redemption #5

<u>Avoiding Temptation</u> #6

<u>Chasing Temptation</u> #7

<u>Rebel Ink Series</u>

<u>Hate You</u> #1

<u>Trick You</u> #2

<u>Defy You</u> #3

<u>Play You</u> #4

<u>Inked</u> (A Rebel Ink/Driven Crossover)

<u>Rosewood High Series</u>

<u>Thorn</u> #1

<u>Paine</u> #2

<u>Savage</u> #3

<u>Fierce</u> #4

<u>Hunter</u> #5

Faze (#6 Prequel)

<u>Fury</u> #6

<u>Legend</u> #7

<u>Maddison Kings University Series</u>

<u>TMYM: Prequel</u>

TRYS #1

TDYW #2

TBYS #3

TVYC #4

TDYD #5

TDYR #6

TRYD #7

Knight's Ridge Empire Series

Wicked Summer Knight: Prequel (Stella & Seb)

Wicked Knight #1 (Stella & Seb)

Wicked Princess #2 (Stella & Seb)

Wicked Empire #3 (Stella & Seb)

Deviant Knight #4 (Emmie & Theo)

Deviant Princess #5 (Emmie & Theo

Deviant Reign #6 (Emmie & Theo)

One Reckless Knight (Jodie & Toby)

Reckless Knight #7 (Jodie & Toby)

Reckless Princess #8 (Jodie & Toby)

Reckless Dynasty #9 (Jodie & Toby)

Dark Halloween Knight (Calli & Batman)

Dark Knight #10 (Calli & Batman)

Dark Princess #11 (Calli & Batman)

Dark Legacy #12 (Calli & Batman)

Corrupt Valentine Knight (Nico & Siren)

Ruined Series

Ruined Plans #1

Ruined by Lies #2

Ruined Promises #3

Never Forget Series

Never Forget Him #1

Never Forget Us #2

Everywhere & Nowhere #3

Chasing Series

Chasing Logan

The Cocktail Girls

His Manhattan

Her Kensington

Tabitha

I stare down at my gran's pale skin. Her cheeks are sunken and her eyes tired. She's been fighting this for too long now, and as much as I hate to even think it, it's time she found some peace.

I take her cool hand in mine and lift her knuckles to my lips.

"It's Tabitha," I whisper. I've no idea if she's awake, but I don't want to startle her.

Her eyes flicker open. After a second they must adjust to the light and she looks right at me. My chest tightens as if someone's wrapping an elastic band around it. I hate seeing my once so full of life gran like this. She was always so happy and full of cheer. She didn't deserve this end. But cancer doesn't care what kind of person you are, it hits whoever it fancies and ruins lives.

Pulling a chair closer, I drop onto it, not taking my eyes from her.

"How are you doing today?" I hate asking the question, because there really is only one answer. She's waiting, waiting for her time to come to put her out of her misery.

"I'm good. Christopher upped my morphine. I'm on top of the world."

She might be living her last days, but it doesn't stop her eyes sparkling a little as she mentions her male nurse. If I've heard the words 'if I were forty years younger' once while she's been here, then I've heard them a million times. She's joking, of course. My gran spent her life with my incredible grandpa until he had a stroke a few years ago. Thankfully, I guess, his end was much quicker and less painful than Gran's. It was awful at the time to have him healthy one moment and then gone in a matter of hours, but this right now is pure torture, and I'm not the one lying on the hospital bed with meds constantly being pumped into my body.

"Turn the frown upside down, Tabby Cat. I'm fine. I want to remember you smiling, not like your world's about to come crashing down."

"I know, I'm sorry. I just—" a sob breaks from my throat. "I don't know how I'm going to live without you." Dramatic? Yeah. But Gran has been my go-to person my whole life. When my parents get on my last nerve, which is often, she's the one who talks me down, makes me see things differently. She's also the only one who's encouraged me to live the life I want, not the one I'm constantly being pushed into.

That's the reason I'm the only one visiting her right now.

When my parents discovered that she was the one encouraging my 'reckless behaviour', as they called it, they cut contact. I can see the pain in her eyes about that every time she looks at me, but she's too stubborn to do anything about it, even now.

"You're going to be fine. You're stronger than you give yourself credit for. How many times have I told you, you just need to follow your heart. Follow your heart and just breathe. Spread your wings and fly, Tabby Cat."

Those were the last words she said to me.

Tabitha

The heavy bass rattles my bones. The incredible music does help to lift my spirits, but I find it increasingly hard to see the positives in my life while I'm hanging out with my friends these days. They've all got something exciting going on—incredible job prospects, marriage, exotic holidays on the horizon—and here I am, drowning in my one-person pity party. It's been two months since Gran left me, and I'm still wondering what the hell I'm meant to be doing with my life.

"Oh my god, they are so fucking awesome,"

Danni squeals in my ear as one song comes to an end. I didn't really have her down as a rock fan, but she was almost as excited as James when he announced that this was what we were doing for his birthday this year. Although I do wonder if it's the music or the frontman who's really captured her attention. She'd never admit it, but she's got a thing for bad boys.

I glance over at him with his arm wrapped around Shannon's shoulders and a smile twitches my lips. They're so cute. They've got the kind of relationship everyone craves. It seems so easy yet full of love and affection. Ripping my eyes from the couple, I focus back on the stage and try to block out that I'm about as far away from having that kind of connection with anyone as physically possible.

I sing along with the songs I've heard on the radio a million times and jump around with my friends, but I just can't quite totally get on board with tonight. Maybe I just need more alcohol.

"Where to next?" Shannon asks once we've left the arena and the ringing in our ears has begun to fade.

"Your choice," James says, looking down at her with utter devotion shining in his eyes. It wasn't a great surprise when Shannon sent a photo of her giant engagement ring to our group chat a couple of months ago. We all knew it was coming—Danni especially, seeing as it turned out that she helped choose the ring.

Shannon directs us all to a cocktail bar a few streets over and I make quick work of manoeuvring my way through the crowd to get to the bar, my need for a drink beginning to get the better of me. The others disappear off somewhere in the hope of finding a table

"Can we have two jugs of..." I quickly glance at the menu. "Margaritas please."

"Coming right up, sweetheart." The barman winks at me before his eyes drop to my chest. Hooking up on a night out isn't really my thing, but hell if it doesn't make me feel a little better about myself. He's cute too, and just the kind of guy who would give both my parents a heart attack if I were to bring him home. Both his forearms are covered in tattoos, he's got gauges in both his ears, and a lip ring. A smile tugs at the corner of my mouth as I imagine the looks on their faces.

My gran's words suddenly hit me.

Just breathe.

My hand lifts and my fingers run over the healing skin just below my bra. My smile widens.

I watch the barman prepare our cocktails, my eyes focused on the ink on his arms. I've always been obsessed by art, any kind of art, and that most definitely includes on skin.

I'm lost in my own head, so when he places the jugs in front of me, I startle, feeling ridiculous.

"T-Thank you," I mutter, but when I lift my eyes, I find him staring intently at me.

"You're welcome. I'm Christian, by the way."

"Oh, hi." A sly smile creeps onto my lips. "I'm Biff."

"Biff?" His brows draw together in a way I'm all too used to when I say my name.

"It's short for Tabitha."

"That's pretty. So... uh... how do you feel about—"

"Christian, a little help?" one of the other barmen shouts, pulling Christian's attention from me.

"Sorry, I'll hopefully see you again later?"

I nod at him, not wanting to give him any false hope. Like I said, he's cute, but after my last string of bad dates and even worse short-term boyfriends, I'm happy flying solo right now. I've got a top of the range vibrating friend in my bedside table; I don't need a man.

Picking up the tray in front of me, I turn and go in search of my friends. It takes forever, but eventually I find them tucked around a tiny table in the back corner of the bar.

"What the hell took so long? We thought you'd pulled and abandoned us."

"Yes and no," I say, ensuring every head turns my way.

"Tell us more," Danni, my best friend, demands.

"It was nothing. The barman was about to ask me out, but it got busy."

"Why the hell did you come back? Get over there. We all know you could do with a little... loosening up," James says with a wink.

"I'm good. He wasn't my type."

"Oh, of course. You only date posh boys."

"That is not true."

"Is it not?" Danni asks, chipping in once she's filled all the glasses.

"No..." I think back over the previous few guys they met. "Wayne wasn't posh," I argue when I realise they're kind of right.

"No, he was just a wanker."

Blowing out a long breath, I try to come up with an argument, but quite honestly, it's true. My shoulders slump as I realise that I've been subconsciously dating guys my parents would approve of. It's like my need to follow their orders is so well ingrained by now that I don't even realise I'm doing it. Shame that their ideas about my life, what I should do, and whom I should date don't exactly line up with mine.

Glancing over my shoulder at the bar, I catch a glimpse of Christian's head. Maybe I should take him up on his almost offer. What's the worst that could happen?

Deciding some liquid courage is in order, I grab my margherita and swallow half down in one go.

I'm so fed up of attempting to live my parents' idea of a perfect life. I promised Gran I'd do things my way. I need to start living up to my promise.

BY THE TIME I'm tipsy enough to walk back to the bar and chat up Christian, he's nowhere to be seen. I'm kind of disappointed seeing as the others had convinced me to throw caution to the wind (something that I'm really bad at doing), but I think

I'm mostly relieved to be able go home and lock myself inside my flat alone and not have to worry about anyone else.

With my arm linked through Danni's, we make our way out to the street, ready to make our journeys home, and Shannon jumps into an idling Uber while Danni waits for another to go in the opposite direction.

"You sure you don't want to be dropped off? I don't mind."

"No, I'm sure. I could do with the fresh air." It's not a lie—the alcohol from one too many cocktails is making my head a little fuzzy. I hate going to sleep with the room spinning. I'd much rather that feeling fade before lying down.

"Okay. Promise me you'll text me when you're home."

"I promise." I wrap my arms around my best friend and then wave her off in her own Uber.

Turning on my heels, I start the short walk home.

I've been a London girl all my life, and while some might be afraid to walk home after dark, I love it. I love seeing a different side to this city, the quiet side when most people are hiding in their flats, not flooding the streets on their daily commutes.

My mind is flicking back and forth between my promise to Gran and my missed opportunity tonight when a shop front that I walk past on almost a daily basis makes me stop.

It's a tattoo studio I've been inside of once in my life. I never really pay it much attention, but the new sign in the window catches my eye and I stop to look.

Admin help wanted. Enquire within.

Something stirs in my belly, and it's not just my need to do something to piss my parents off— although getting a job in a place like this is sure to do that. I'm pretty sure it's excitement.

Tattoos fascinate me, or more so, the artists.

I'm surprised to see the open sign still illuminated, so before I can change my mind, I push the door open. A little bell rings above it, and after a few seconds of standing in reception alone, a head pops out from around the door.

"Evening. What can I do you for?" The guy's smile is soft and kind despite his otherwise slightly harsh features and ink.

"Oh um..." I hesitate under his intense dark stare. I glance over my shoulder, the back of the piece of paper catching my eye and reminding me why I walked in here. "I just saw the job ad in the window. Is the position still open?"

His eyes drop from mine and take in what I'm wearing. Seeing as tonight's outing involved a rock concert, I'm dressed much like him in all black and looking a little edgy with my skinny black jeans, ripped AC/DC t-shirt and heavy black makeup. I must admit it's not a look I usually go for, but it was fitting for tonight.

He nods, apparently happy with what he sees.

"Experience?" he asks, making my stomach drop.

"Not really, but I'm studying for a Masters so I'm not an idiot. I know my way around a computer, Excel, and I'm super organised."

"Right..." he trails off, like he's thinking about the best way to get rid of me.

"I'm a really quick learner. I'm punctual, methodical and really easy to get along with."

"It's okay, you had me sold at organised. I'm Dawson, although everyone around here calls me D."

"Nice to meet you." I stick my hand out for him to shake, and an amused smile plays at his lips. Stretching out an inked arm, he takes my hand and gives it a very firm shake that my dad would be impressed by—if he could look past the tattoos, that is. "I'm Tabitha, but everyone calls me Biff."

"Biff, I like it. When can you start?"

"Don't you want to interview me?"

"You sound like you could be perfect. When can you start?"

"Err... tomorrow?" I ask, totally taken aback. He doesn't know me from Adam.

"Yes!" He practically snaps my hand off. "Can you be here for two o'clock? I can show you around before clients start turning up. I'll apologise now for dropping you in the deep end, we've not had anyone for a few weeks and things are starting to get a little crazy."

"I can cope with crazy."

"Good to know. This place can be nuts." I smile at him, more grateful than he could know to have a distraction and a focus.

My Masters should be enough to keep my mind busy, but since Gran went, I can't seem to lose myself in it like I could previously. Hopefully, sorting this place's admin out might be exactly what I need.

"Two o'clock tomorrow then," I say, turning to leave. "I'll bring ID. Do you need a reference? I've done some voluntary work recently, I'm sure they'll write something for me."

"Just turn up on time and do your job and you're golden."

I walk out with more of a spring in my step than I have in a long time. I'm determined to find something that's going to make me happy, not just my parents. I've lived in their shadow for long enough.

I LOOK myself over before leaving my flat for my first shift at the tattoo studio. I'm dressed a little more like myself today in a pair of dark skinny jeans, a white blouse and a black blazer. It's simple and smart. I'm not sure if there's a dress code—D never specified what I should wear. With my hair straightened and hanging down my back and my makeup light, I feel like I can take on whatever crazy he throws at me.

With a final spritz of perfume, I grab my bag from the unit in the hall and pull open my door. My home is a top floor flat in an old London warehouse. They were converted a few years ago by my father's company, and I managed to get myself first dibs. They might drive me insane on the best of days, but at least I get this place rent-free. It almost makes up for their controlling and stuck-up ways... almost.

Ignoring the lift like I always do, I head for the stairs. My heels click against the polished concrete until I'm at the bottom and out to the busy city. I love London. I love that no matter what the time, there's always something going on or someone who's awake.

The spring afternoon is still a little fresh, making me regret not grabbing my coat, or even a scarf, before I left. I pull my blazer tighter around myself and make the short journey to the shop.

The door's locked when I get there, and the bright neon sign that clearly showed it was open last night is currently saying closed.

Unsure of what to do, I lift my hand to knock. Only a second later, the shop front is illuminated, and the sound of movement inside filters down to me, but when the door opens it's not the guy from last night.

"Oh... uh... hi. Is... uh... D here?"

The guy folds his arms over his chest and looks me up and down. He chuckles, although I've no idea what he finds so amusing.

"D," he shouts over his shoulder, "there's some posh bird here to see you."

My teeth grind that he's stereotyped me quite so quickly, but I refuse to allow him to see that his assumptions about me affect me in any way.

"Ah, good. I was worried you might change your mind."

"Not at all," I say, stepping past the judgemental arsehole and into the studio reception-cum-waiting room.

"That's Spike. Feel free to ignore him. He's not got laid in about a million years, it makes him a little cranky." I fight to contain a laugh, especially when I turn toward Spike to find his lips pursed and his eyes narrowed in frustration. All it does is confirm that D's words are correct.

"Is that fucking necessary? Posh doesn't need to know how inactive my cock is, especially not when she's only just walked through the fucking door. Unless..." He stalks towards me and I automatically back up. I can't deny that he's a good looking guy, but there's no way I'm going there.

"I don't think so."

"You sure? You look like you could do with a bit of rough." He winks, and I want the ground to swallow me up.

"Down, Spike. This is Tabitha, or Biff. She's our new admin, so I suggest you be nice to her if you want to stop organising your own appointments and shit. I don't need a sexual harassment case on my hands before she's even fucking started."

I can't help but laugh at the look on Spike's face. "Don't worry. I'm sure you'll find some desperate old spinster soon."

He looks me up and down again, something in his eyes changed. "Appearances aside, I think you're going to get on well here."

I smile at him. "Mine's a coffee. Milk, no sugar. I'm already sweet enough." His chin drops.

"I thought you were our new assistant. Why am I still making the coffee?"

"Know your place, Spike. Now do as the lady says. You know my order."

"Yeah, it comes with a side of fuck off!" He flips D off before disappearing through a door that I can only assume goes to a kitchen.

"I probably should have warned you that you've agreed to work around a bunch of arseholes."

"I know how to handle myself around horny men, don't worry."

After finishing my A levels, before I grew any kind of backbone where my parents were concerned, I agreed to work for my dad. I was his little office bitch and spent an horrendous year of my life being bossed around by men who thought that just because they had a cock hanging between their legs it made them better than me. I might have fucking hated that year, but it taught me a few things, not just about business but also how to deal with men who think they're something fucking special just because they're a tiny bit successful and make more money than me. I've no doubt that my time at Anderson Development Group gave me all the skills I'm going to need to handle these artists.

"So I see. So, this is your desk. When you're on shift you'll be the first person people see when they're inside, so it's important that you look good. But from what I've seen, I don't think we'll have an issue. I've sorted you out logins for the computer and the software we use. Most of it is pretty self-explanatory. I'm pretty IT illiterate and I've figured most of it out, put it that way."

D's showing me how they book clients in when someone else joins us. This time it's someone I recognise from my previous visit, although it's immediately obvious that he doesn't remember me like I do him. But then I guess he was the one delivering the pain, not receiving it.

"Biff, this is Titch. Titch, this is Biff, our new admin. Be nice."

"Nice? I'm always nice. Nice to meet you, Biff. You have any issues with this one, you come and see me. He might look tough, but I know all his secrets." Titch winks, a smile curling at his lips that shows he's a little more interested than he's making out, and quickly disappears towards his room.

It's not long until the first clients of the afternoon arrive, and I'm left alone to try to get to grips with everything.

Between clients, D pops his head out of his room to check I'm okay, and every hour I make a round of coffee for everyone. That sure seems to get me in their good books.

"I think I could get used to having you around," Spike says when I deliver probably his fourth coffee of the day. "Only thing that would make it better is if it were whisky."

"Not sure the person at the end of your needle would agree." He chuckles and turns back to the design he was working on when I interrupted.

My first day flies by. D tells me to head home

not long after nine o'clock. They've all got hours of tattooing to go yet, seeing as Saturday night is their busiest night of the week, but he insists I get a decent night's sleep.

ONE-CLICK to continue reading.

www.ingramcontent.com/pod-product-compliance
Lightning Source LLC
Chambersburg PA
CBHW061552210726
48287CB00006B/2158